PRAISE FOR

*Miss Manhattan*

"Stephen Wolf intertwines historical fiction with a contemporary street-smart detective story to create a totally enjoyable read with prose that creates vivid images. Simply the best book I've read in quite a while."

—Michael Nupuf, author of the play *Accolade to Audrey*

"Kudos to Stephen Wolf for reviving the legacy of Audrey Munson—the forgotten icon, mistreated muse, and America's first supermodel—with compassion, vivid storytelling, and literary grace. By rescuing her from historical obscurity, Wolf not only restores Munson's rightful place in popular culture but also makes a significant contribution to the recognition of women in art history."

—Michael J. Coffino, author of the multi-award-winning *Truth Is in the House*

"Stephen Wolf brings turn-of-the-century New York to vibrant life in this fascinating and absorbing story of the model Audrey Munson and the modern artist who seeks to find her. Beautifully observed and told."

—Mark Mustian, author of *The Gendarme* and *Boy with Wings*

"A luminous and evocative novel, *Miss Manhattan* masterfully intertwines history and art, bringing to life the extraordinary story of Audrey Munson—the muse behind some of New York's most iconic statues.

With lyrical prose and vivid detail, Stephen Wolf captures the spirit of a bygone New York, illuminating the triumphs and tragedies of a woman both immortalized and forgotten. This story is beautifully written, a must-read for lovers of historical fiction and art alike."

—Lacy Fewer, author of *Yankeeland*

"Stephen Wolf's lush prose brings Audrey Munson from stone to life in this finely drawn work that evokes her yearnings as well as the toll of collective desire on a young muse. In a time when New York City glimmered with promise just as the global clouds of war rolled in, Audrey's hope and tragedy came to echo an era. Wolf also invites us on a search for answers in a more modern day, as a young artist scours the city to uncover the story behind the statues. The twining of these accounts captures the passion, inspiration, and sense of quest when one is deeply moved by a work of art. Without question, *Miss Manhattan* should be read now, widely, and for a long time for the worlds it resurrects and creates."

—Sean Akerman, author of *Outposts*, *Krakow*, and *The Fields*

"Stephen Wolf's tender, delightful novel brings to vivid life one of the most fascinating yet little-known figures of New York history—Audrey Munson, the 'Queen of the Artists' Studio'—briefly one of the most famous women in the city before World War I, who then spent decades lingering in obscurity in a mental institution. Wolf handles this fascinating tale with brio, vivid and evocative prose, and a revelatory vision. *Miss Manhattan* is at once a love letter to New York, an exploration of the creative spirit of artists and the models who inspire them, and a tour de force of novelistic time travel. For anyone interested in the city, art, and love, *Miss Manhattan* should not be missed."

—Daniel J. Wakin, author of *The Man with the Sawed-Off Leg and Other Tales of a New York City Block*

"Audrey Munson, 'the world's most perfectly formed woman' who modeled for some of NYC's best-loved statues, is no longer a well-known name, but Stephen Wolf's novel brings her back to life, a life intimately intertwined with the history of New York City itself. In addition, there is NYC in the 1990s with Sophia as a modern artist whose life choices mirror Audrey's. Such are a few of the numerous delights readers will derive from this astutely observed novel."

—Louis Phillips. author of *The Ballroom in Saint Patrick's Cathedral*

"Stephen Wolf's *Miss Manhattan* is a sweet page-turner that celebrates New York's underappreciated Audrey Munson. She has only recently been discovered as the model for the city's best outdoor masterpieces. Worthy of cult status, Wolf weaves her amazing life into a page-turning story that covers and connects a full century. What a delightful historical novel! And what a fun educational tool as well!"

—Jim Makin, the author of *Notable New Yorkers of Manhattan's Upper West Side, Bloomingdale-Morningside Heights*

"Whether an informed enthusiast of enduring art or an intrigued novice, the reader will not soon forget the story of Audrey Munson, a stunning young model whose figure graces many of New York City's most iconic landmarks. Wolf deftly volleys between past and present in his narrative of 'the great city's queen,' who lived on the cusp of New York's prewar art scene yet fell into obscurity far too quickly. *Miss Manhattan* is an extraordinary reminder of both the lasting grip of art upon our world and the inconstancy of life itself."

—Brenda Massman, author of *Yet, Here We Are*

*Miss Manhattan*
by Stephen Wolf

© Copyright 2025 Stephen Wolf

979-8-88824-682-5

All rights reserved. No part of this publication may be reproduced, stored in a retrieval system, or transmitted in any form or by any means—electronic, mechanical, photocopy, recording, or any other—except for brief quotations in printed reviews, without the prior written permission of the author.

This is a work of fiction. The characters may be both actual and fictitious. With the exception of verified historical events and persons, all incidents, descriptions, dialogue, and opinions expressed are the products of the author's imagination and are not to be construed as real.

Illustrations by David Joel (www.davidjoelart.com)
*Three Graces*, 2024 © 2025 David Joel
*Memory*, 2024 © 2025 David Joel
*Daphne*, 2024 © 2025 David Joel
*Miss Manhattan*, 2024 © 2025 David Joel

Cover design by Suzanne Bradshaw.

Published by
◣ köehlerbooks™

3705 Shore Drive
Virginia Beach, VA 23455
800-435-4811
www.koehlerbooks.com

# MISS MANHATTAN

a novel

## STEPHEN WOLF

VIRGINIA BEACH
CAPE CHARLES

"Where is she now, this model who was so beautiful?"
—Audrey Munson, May 1, 1921

## *Prologue*

One mild afternoon late in May, a plump squirrel leaps from a branch of a linden tree to a second-story window ledge where a peanut lays. Snatching it up and rolling it between its tiny paws before stuffing the peanut in its mouth, jowls bulging, the squirrel hops back to the branch and scampers up the tree. Shell and shuck soon drift down, then the squirrel returns along the branch just as a woman's thin, pale hand places another peanut on the window ledge.

Her long hair is whiter than her face of few wrinkles owing to a long lifetime of shielding herself from sunlight under brimmed hats, that and her daily ritual even to this day; her fingertips dab milk drops around her lips, across her forehead and cheeks and down her throat as her blue-gray eyes raise to a jet liner high above, audible despite the great distance.

At the far end of the hospital ward, away from the old woman and the resourceful squirrel, a quiet gathering of several people around an old woman in bed, a small package in her lap.

"Oh thank you" and "How pretty" and "Open it Granma" which she does with arthritic hands ringless and unsteady. Beneath the pink ribbon and white wrapping paper, a finely polished wood box for precious items—a locket, a bracelet of hair, a silver dollar from a special year. When opened, the box plays the first sweet, metallic notes of "The

Sidewalks of New York" as the melody's haunting little two-step drifts above the clean linoleum floor, and beds covered in white cotton spreads with their dozing patients. The melody slows, expending as it drifts by the partitioned utility stations and the hushed steps of the attendant nurses towards the distant, sunlit window where the old woman, apprehensive but smiling faintly, turns to the fading, soft notes from the music box.

# Chapter One

Kittie sat on the edge of her daughter's bed fussing lightly with the blanket and asked with a faint smile to the uncertainty in Audrey's eyes, "Nervous about tomorrow, are you?"

After a deep breath and several quick nods, Audrey whispered, "A little."

With her fingertips Kittie delicately moved a single, long strand of black hair from Audrey's forehead to behind her ear.

"Well you needn't be worryin'," she said while fussing with the blanket again. "You've a lovely figure and there's—"

"Oh it's not that," her voice hushed and urgent. "But that *way*," she laughed nervously, "in front of him."

Kittie hurried this away with a light laugh and renewed soft pats to the blanket.

"Your friend Rozie says he is a great artist with statues at world exhibitions and in a church downtown and something for that poor president assassinated but a few years ago," and leans closer. "He's seen many models in the" and she sat back again, pouting. "What did he call it?"

With whispered hesitancy, Audrey uttered, "The altogether."

"Yes," and Kittie laughed, "the altogether."

The small flame from the gaslight flickered in Audrey's pensive eyes, but Kittie assured her "and I'll be right there to be sure you're not compromised."

In quiet amazement Audrey whispered, "He said it is to be the centerpiece for a great celebration honoring Henry Hudson and Robert Fulton." A single, deep crease appeared between her lowered eyes. "And there's to be three figures."

Her anxiety increasing, she again looked at her mother. "Am I to pose in the altogether for all *three*?"

Kittie rose from the bed while saying, "Now don't fret about this tonight. And remember you needn't do anything you won't be wantin' to do," and she nodded with finality, "even if he's payin' us more than you're makin' with the Dancin' Dolls."

After kissing her daughter's forehead again and while lowering the gas-flame, Kittie said, "All you need do is imagine you're on stage," adding flippantly, "that you're acting," then left the door open enough for a thin line of sharp light to fall across the floor of the dark room.

Audrey lay in bed worrying about tomorrow but ever grateful for her mother's protective wing. Kittie had taken her only child away from Audrey's father because of his infidelities, and that Edgar Munson married "this German, Cora Cook," Kittie would later snarl, only added to her humiliation. With her six-year-old by the hand she fled Rochester for Providence, Rhode Island, where a cousin lived amid a large Irish population, and now, to their wonderment, here they were in New York City where Audrey lay in bed listening to the night sounds out her window. Horse-hooves clomped along a cobblestone street; a clattering wagon; a distant, rattling engine of a motor car; water running through the pipes of the apartment above. *Will there be other men at the studio?* she wondered. *His assistants?* Again she was grateful her mother would be with her.

Summoning her courage after a deep breath, Audrey slipped from bed and stood in the center of the dark room. After another, deeper breath, she loosened the tie of her nightgown that fell in flannel wrinkles to her feet. She felt chilly air on her naked body and after a moment grew self-conscious; her heartbeat quickened, and she shut her eyes. She breathed deeply several times, tightened her fists with determination, then opened her eyes, only to again shut them as she imagined Konti gazing at her. After several deep breaths, with chin uplifted, she opened her eyes for an instant until once more she panicked at the vulnerability of her own nakedness. *Perhaps,* she admitted, *I can't do this after all, that I'll keep performing with the Dancin' Dolls until I'm a Ziegfeld Girl* like she'd been hoping since the time she worried if it were a sin that during daily prayers at Saint Francis Xavier Academy she had wished to become a star.

In his firm, polite, Austrian resolve, Isidore Konti declared that Audrey must be willing to pose "in the altogether" to Kittie's instant indignation. He slowly turned from Audrey's uncertainty and told Kittie that "Every beautiful woman must contribute what she can to art and loveliness." With another deep breath, resolute, Audrey thought of herself not as herself but a graceful statue she'd once seen in a cemetery, and there was that photograph of a painting in a magazine –a naked woman standing upright in a seashell; *surely someone posed for these*. She opened her eyes, heartbeat simmering, her breath steady now. Thinking of herself as the woman in the seashell and the one who posed for the grave, she bent her knees slightly, and in her nakedness she extended her arms, modesty dispelled, reaching with palms upturned to the magic city beyond the black window.

LEAVING EARLY THE next morning for Isidore Konti's studio, Audrey and Kittie rode for a nickel each the streetcar from 91st Street down Broadway. This hilly part of the island teemed with small farms raising pigs, tomatoes, and children. There were rows of low, wood apartment buildings, a church steeple in the distance to the east, the sound of a blacksmith's hammer, and immense horses exhaling great clouds of breath on chilly mornings while pulling wagonloads of chopped wood, coal, and bundles of newspapers heaved to the sidewalk. Further down

Broadway, markets opened as striped awnings unrolled over wooden bins of cabbage and potatoes, onions and apples. The city grew denser as the day brightened along with Audrey's excitement at each block further downtown. The great variety enthralled her as more people appeared on the sidewalks now. Crimson-brick buildings pressed side-by-side, and a double-decker omnibus rumbled with uncertainty; to Audrey's distress, here the few, thin horses were beset by car horns, bus bells, and motorcars black and wobbling, yet the continual, pandering parade of people on the sidewalks thrilled her each day.

Konti's large studio with tall, hazy windows covered half of the top floor in the Lincoln Arcade Building on Broadway near West 66th Street. On wood platforms stood cloth-covered sculptures in plaster or clay in various stages of completion, dust floating in the bright air before settling on everything. Middle-age, robust, his mustache and goatee trimmed— and one of New York's most renowned sculptors— Isidore Konti knew that his three graces will pose not upright as do Canova's and Raphael's and Botticelli's but reclining as Phidias had done two thousand years before. He made many sketches of Audrey lounging on a long sofa wearing a flowing chiton, her left arm on a cushion, then her right, her head turned to one side, then the other, page after sketch pad page tossed to the cement floor, then she bares a shoulder while Kittie hovered protectively nearby.

Kittie was proud at Audrey's rising success, for it had been Kittie who encouraged the girl's dancing at the St. Francis Academy where she'd enrolled Audrey once they moved from Rochester to Providence. At the all-girls academy, Audrey would absorb good religious training but also be kept from the provocations of boys. Even then Kittie imagined how Audrey's talent might prove profitable, and after soon realizing that posing was Konti's only intention with her daughter she stayed home rather than making the arduous journey twice daily and saving two nickels besides.

Audrey proved to be a fine model. She was punctual, had a pleasant disposition, took directions well, and seemingly tireless as she shifted positions—"Turn your head the other way," Konti said—and attitudes—

"as if you're looking in the distance"—though she found holding a pose difficult after only a few minutes. *How much different to lounge on a sofa,* she laughed to herself, instead of rehearsing repeatedly until the feet of some girls bled. Still, she enjoyed performing at the small theater with the gay applause, spotlights, and playful piano music where she dreamed of dancing on Broadway wearing a gorgeous gown rather than those silly, ruffled skirts.

Now she found herself rather bored in a vast, dreary loft—"Lower your arm"— but earning more money posing on a sofa than from those exhausting rehearsals.

Late one morning Konti laid down his sketch pad and Audrey changed from the light garment back to her shirtwaist and tapered skirt and always a hat with a brim. Together they rode in a black carriage along a transverse road slightly beneath Central Park to the Metropolitan Museum of Art on Fifth Avenue. Never had Audrey ridden in a carriage with its red leather seats and the steady pattern of the horse's hooves, and again she felt as if she were rising a little higher in this city of impossibilities.

"To be a fine model," Konti declared as the green park passed outside the window, "you must know sculpture."

He decried the poor quality of public sculptures in New York, saying, "In Paris we'd need only stroll the Luxembourg Gardens to see beautiful artwork," then added a little unhappily, "but Paris is an artist's city."

Politely but with protective affection, Audrey asked, "Isn't New York an artist's city?"

Konti turned from the window, then after a moment, "Perhaps a different type of artist," and his spirit lightened. "It is too soon to tell."

He assisted her from the carriage, and the sight of the museum that seemed to her more like a palace dazzled her with its cranberry-colored stone, its tall columns, arched windows above the entrance. Across from it, the magnificent homes on Fifth Avenue. Inside the museum, the vast lobby with its lofty ceiling and lavish bouquets in large vases on each side of a great staircase. Never had she known that there were such places nor that anyone may enter them, even a girl from Rochester.

"We begin with the Greeks," Konti said decidedly.

They strolled the quiet galleries where paintings hung in elaborate frames and with small sculptures in glass cases and large ones on stone pedestals. In other galleries, huge statues in granite, some missing arms or heads; here Konti paused before a life-size figure of a seated boy, parts of him missing too.

"Everything about him is focused on the same purpose," Konti told her slowly. "His rounded shoulders, his intense gaze, the left hand holding his foot that has a thorn, his careful right hand."

She bent to see the boy's face, nose and a portion of his chin missing.

"No matter," Konti continued, "that the foot with the thorn and his hand trying to remove it were lost centuries ago. What endures is that every part of him tells the story."

Audrey thought of the boy who had posed for it, a boy who had died very long ago but now with a statue of him here in New York City. She realized with a small jolt that what she was posing for, this statue of three lounging sisters, might too live as long as this Greek boy. The idea seemed as impossible as plucking a star from the sky, but here was this Greek boy upon whom she gazed on a quiet afternoon a thousand years later. *Could such things ever come true?* Her breath quickened at the possibility.

"Any capable craftsmen can carve a hand," Konti said as they resumed their stroll, "but a true artist puts expression into each finger,"

Konti stopped abruptly before a statue of three women on a pedestal, each one shapely, trim, slightly smaller than life-size, upright, armless, headless, with two of the figures facing her, the center one with its back to her, and all three were nude.

"Is this familiar?" he asked, smiling slightly. "We are part of a tradition, you and I, over three thousand years old. Perhaps *our* Three Graces will last so long."

Gazing at the figures, Audrey imagined a little fearfully posing in the same way, upright and nude. She felt embarrassed even now completely dressed beside Konti with the naked figures before them. Her uncertainty returned, and she wondered with renewed trepidation if she could ever do this. *Perhaps Mommy can accompany me again until the posing ends?*

They continued through other galleries, Konti returning a polite nod to those who nod to him. Dazzled again that she was allowed to roam freely in the galleries' quiet sanctity—passed the beautiful paintings in elaborate frames, the sculptures close enough to touch—Audrey felt the kind of holy aura she'd felt in church.

"Venus and Adonis," Konti said to the canvas of Rubens' lusty figures in their final embrace before the handsome lover's fateful hunt; with a small shock Audrey saw that Venus too was naked. "And The Judgement of Paris," and Konti pointed to a painting with *three* naked women, but Audrey wasn't listening carefully how "each goddess will grant" but instead thinking *must I pose* "as a bribe for the apple" *like these women?* She knew *some*one had posed for them, *but could I?*

"And now, Miss Munson," he said with light formality, "will you join me for lunch?"

Again she rode in a carriage but this time down Fifth Avenue with magnificent mansions to one side in golden, afternoon sunlight and Central Park's tall row of elm trees to the other. In the Oak Room of the Plaza Hotel, the two sat down at a table with sparkling silverware and China plates edged with a delicate floral design, and here too abundant flower bouquets. Audrey smiled quietly while telling herself, *I'm not dreaming . . . this is not a dream.*

"Isidore," declared a tall, portly, tuxedoed man, "how good to see you."

"Henry," Konti replied, and they shook hands. "Your hotel looks wonderful."

Henry gazed forlornly at the pastel-colored walls, upward to the high ceiling and the oval skylight.

"She's not the Ritz," he said before smiling broadly, "but she's younger and more beautiful" as he turned to Audrey.

"Henry Black," Konti said, "Miss Audrey Munson."

He bowed slightly. "Miss Munson, a pleasure, and are you a model?"

"The finest," Konti declared, and Audrey's heart surged with pride for an instant, then she nodded gratefully to him.

"Then perhaps," Henry Black said to her, "you can persuade Mr. Konti to create a statue for outside my hotel."

"Henry," Konti sighed exasperated and amused, "I told you Karl Bitter is your man. Such a work will need a basin, tiers, and a grand fountain. I am a simple sculptor, not a city planner."

"Well, we must decide soon," Henry Black uttered irritably. "Since General Sherman arrived the Vanderbilts want a statue of the Commodore outside their gate." He shook his head, dismayed. "Imagine a statue of Cornelius Vanderbilt in front of my hotel."

Quickly revived, he turned again to Audrey. "Miss Munson, a pleasure to meet you, and perhaps one day *your* figure will appear outside my hotel."

After a slight bow Henry Black strode to other guests. In time he would get what he desired before the Vanderbilts could raise a statue of the Commodore and sculpted by Karl Bitter, as Konti had suggested. It would be of Pomona, naked, demurely holding a basket filled with the plentiful harvest above the basins only steps from the lavish doors of the Plaza Hotel. But the goddess was still unfinished one early April night in 1915 after Bitter and his wife left the Metropolitan Opera House; a taxi had jumped the curb moments before Bitter pushed his wife to safety, though he was struck and killed. His friend Isidore Konti would complete the statue meant for the Pulitzer Fountain, Audrey posing for it.

Following perfectly grilled salmon, roasted potatoes with asparagus, during tea and a choice of French pastries served on a gleaming silver tray, Konti told Audrey about the Michelangelo he'd seen in the Louvre.

"A captive slave, larger than life, a hand to his chest," and Konti placed his hand slightly free from his shirt-buttons. "I was young and bold and somehow found the audacity to approach the statue that I might look underneath the hand."

He sipped his tea, then, quietly, "The palm had been carved with lines and ridges," and he shook his head, amazed even after many years.

"But why?" Audrey asked. "Who would," and she laughed lightly, "besides you—"

"God could see," Konti replied immediately and leaned closer. "It is the entire body that tells the story, every detail, even the smallest."

He reached across the table to take her hand.

"How you place each finger," he said, "that too must reveal the soul of the piece," and pressed her hand, his eyes remaining in hers. "Everything must tell the story."

Listening, absorbed, Audrey nodded understandingly. *Everything must tell the story*, she told herself, then Konti released her hand, sat back in his cushioned chair and sighed.

Beneath the hotel's ornate canopy he pointed ahead to his right; there Henry Black wanted the figure and fountain to rise just in front of the tall, black iron gates that to Audrey protected a palace. She remembered this mansion and those iron gates when first walking Fifth Avenue with her mother in those dreamy weeks after first arriving in New York. She had marveled that one family—American royalty—actually lived there and remembered seeing the three young people, a slender woman and two trim men, each bright and eager, entering their sparkling city through these tall iron gates.

"Take the young lady wherever she desires," Konti said from the sidewalk to the coachman once Audrey settled in the carriage. "It has been delightful," he told her, tipping his derby, "and I will see you in the morning."

"Thank you for this day," she said with deep gratitude as he closed the carriage door.

"We shall have others like it," he promised as the carriage trotted on. "There is much to learn."

The carriage wound along the roadway of Central Park as Audrey laughed faintly how that morning she rode to Konti's studio on a streetcar but returned home like this! The roadway through the park was winding and hilly, the park outside the carriage window such a wonderful blend of forest and the city too with its strolling people. She wondered how much the ride cost and if people in the park believed that the carriage belonged to her, a Broadway star perhaps or daughter of an entitled family. And though jubilant from her excursion to the museum and lunch at the gorgeous hotel, she thought again of what she'd seen in the galleries, and her heartbeat quickened with another surge of fear at the nudes. She recalled Konti's words that everything tells the story, all of her, and through the steady *clop . . . clop* of the horse's hooves said aloud, "Even my little finger," as she once more felt blessed by some special, fated grace guiding her path as surely as did this carriage coachman.

"This will do fine, please," Audrey said to him. For the next twenty minutes, she gazed through books on wooden trays outside a small, dim shop among a half-block of small, dim shops up Broadway. For a dime she purchased a used copy of *Great Statues of the World,* and that night, after delicately, customarily, patting milk-drops on her cheeks, her throat and forehead and around her lips, Audrey remained at the table gazing at the photographs in her new, used book.

Like the museum that day, "We begin with the Greeks," Audrey said. *Venus de Milo* with a face Audrey thought not beautiful but handsome though her naked breasts were beautiful, and her naked belly, and the tilt in her hip to where her garment fell. She wondered how the missing arms had been placed and the way she herself would pose them. On the next page, a headless woman in a flowing garment, her wings opened behind her, and a trim, naked man coiled to throw a discus, then the handsome, naked *David.* She gazed upon the figure, upright and relaxed though his face seemed concerned. She marveled that a young man could pose so comfortably this way, then giggled while imagining the great Michelangelo carving a penis. On the next page, the most beautiful statue she'd ever seen.

"Mommy come here," and both women gazed on the dead Christ lying across his mother's lap. "How can a man carve such a thing?" Audrey whispered. "What means *Pieta*?" though Kittie didn't know either; she'll ask Mr. Konti tomorrow.

As an artist's model now, she thought of the woman—Mother

Mary, she knew, but couldn't imagine how someone could pose as the Madonna, taking the weight of her dead son, Jesus, supine across her legs. When she could think beyond the statue's beautifully rendered sorrow, Audrey saw the figures now as models posing four-hundred years ago in Michelangelo's studio. She wondered how she'd feel with a handsome, nearly naked man lying in her lap and if she were capable then of truly imagining who the model represented, the mother of God. *Everything must tell the story*, she told herself again. *Especially my heart and soul.*

She lingered on their hands. Mary's left hand extended slightly outward, her palm upturned as if in giving. Her other hand supported her son beneath his lifeless arm, and Audrey's heart ached at the portion of his mother's garment between his first and second finger, as if he were still holding on.

She turned the next few pages of the book, glancing at a young man running and nearly grasping a young woman, half of her a tree. Then a seated, sturdy, naked man in thought though at first Audrey imagined him sitting on a commode, but her mind was not on statues now. She again felt and with renewed conviction that her destiny was entwined with this marvelous city that had called for her and had taken her in, that she had left her girlhood and now relented her earlier path to what she felt a greater power, and to her faith in this guiding spirit she would surrender all herself.

∽

EVEN BEFORE A New York tabloid declared her "The Most Perfectly Formed Woman in the World" Audrey knew she'd been blessed with beauty for which she took good care as if given a valuable, irreplaceable gift. Make-up, she believed, was for actresses or fashion photographs only, and she faithfully performed her nightly ritual of dabbing milk above and below her lips, in soft circles on both cheeks, her forehead, and along her throat, all for a pure complexion. With King Gilette's new

Milady Décolléte safety razor she made smooth the flesh under her arms and down her legs, and one night each week she coated her long hair with olive oil where it remained for an hour before shampooing. She wore shoes only with a slight heel to preserve the fine form of her ankles and feet—soon to be immortalized in a tribute to love—no garters because of the unsightly imprint made on a thigh, and never a corset except in the chorus line; not only was one uncomfortable but Audrey believed a woman's figure needn't be held in place with whale bone.

She avoided the temptations and exotic lifestyle renowned among the New York theater and artists' world gathering in dark nightclubs with seductive jazz and promises of pleasure not because of her Catholic school days nor her mother's protective wing but knowing such nights and the stimulants to enhance them would quickly harm her complexion, her figure, and her ability to pose for as long as the artist needed. She knew that her breasts—neither large nor small and slightly upturned—the roundness of her bottom, the two dimples above it—which later, she believed, proved more valuable than government bonds—her thighs neither too full nor too thin, her knees not boney, and her well-proportioned calves, slender ankles, and delicate feet were gifts from Mother Nature, good fortune, and care.

After another week of posing in the chilly, sunless studio Audrey and Konti revisited the museum as she shook her head in quiet amazement during the carriage ride that she was paid while doing such a wondrous thing. The large, brown building looked just as stately as weeks earlier, the bouquets in the lobby as abundant, the paintings in silent galleries unchanged, then she realized with a small, thrilling rush of her blood that she wasn't only viewing artwork anymore but had become a participant, adding to its creation, a membership in this ancient and exclusive company, that *I too am an artist*.

Konti paused before a painting of a nude woman on a pedestal seen from the back; a man embraces her, and where their lips touch a pink flush emanates through her flesh.

"A wonderful story," Konti said quietly, "an artist in love with his own work. Gérôme did another version, a frontal view but chose to exhibit this instead. Here is added mystery."

While escorting Audrey by the elbow to the next gallery, he whispered urgently, "And there lies the unmatched power of sculpture. There *is* no mystery. We circle the piece, gaze only inches away, even run our hands along it. Everything revealed," he said emphatically, "nothing hidden," and he paused before a life-size figure in bronze of a naked, standing man. Audrey was mildly shocked at the sight of him so exposed and vulnerable and real.

"Here is no story," Konti told her. "And cast only in bronze since marble would idealize him."

Konti gazed at the statue a while, his eyes traveling along the full form of the lean figure. Audrey too glanced once but quickly at the entire man before focusing on the right hand grasping the top of his head as if in anguish.

"He is so realistic," Konti said, "the artist was accused of not sculpting at all but making casts of a man's body. And *never* could Rodin do such a work," as he looked at Audrey, "without a model who trusted him enough to pose this way. A young Belgian soldier, Auguste Neyt," then his gaze returned to *The Age of Bronze*.

"Only because he revealed himself so completely," Konti said, "could this be created, otherwise there's a fine statue with no spirit, what Shakespeare called a face without a heart."

Cautiously Audrey's eyes moved along the dark figure—the toned torso, his bent knee not turned protectively inward, his limp, fragile penis, and he stands so vulnerable and exposed in spite of it.

The next morning she was nervous in Konti's studio. She changed into the light gown before taking various poses on the sofa as he circled her and sketching all the while, her arms free from her body. Audrey closed her eyes, her heart beating rapidly, then imagined herself as a statue already complete—that and the young Belgian soldier—before letting the thin straps of the light garment fall from her shoulders and down her breasts; it was like leaping into chilly water—at first a shock but then exhilarating. She felt aroused and softly breathed through her mouth, her heartbeat surging, then the garment fell lower, down the pale, smooth slope of her belly to between her legs.

# Chapter Two

On the warmest March 15 ever recorded in New York City—77 degrees in 1990— Sophia sits in the dark on a four-foot-long section of a tree among other cleanly sliced sections of that tree on the forest floor deep in the North Woods of Central Park. While rolling a cigarette she hears the squeaking wheels of a hand truck along the walkway, then Terry instantly hears the click from her opening a Zippo lighter and sees its flame bright in the darkness.

"There," he whispers to Pete as they push into the woods where leaves crunch and twigs snap.

"This is the middle of Man*hattan*?" Pete declares, hushed and amazed.

Sophia watches as they near, exhales a puff into the night, then, "Hi Terry, hi Petie."

Terry gazes at the piece of the tree where Sophia sits, nodding several times before asking, "And you're sure she's in there?"

"She's in there," and hops off the log as Terry leans for a brief kiss.

Quick, efficient, Terry and Pete heave the section of log upright and secure it with a cord to the hand truck which they push and lug to the walkway and back to the road where the truck waits, the *tick-tick* of its emergency lights growing louder. The tailgate raises, the lift lowers, the log is loaded onto the truck and secured to its side panel, then the airbrakes disengage with a *whoosh*. With Terry, Sophia, and Pete in the cab, the old truck rumbles along the winding, hilly roadway.

"It's beautiful here," Pete yells above the loud engine, then Terry flicks off the headlights and the roadway vanishes.

"Terry!" Sophia cries.

They clatter and rumble down Second Avenue to Houston Street, left to First Avenue, then a quick left on East 1st Street. Terry eases the truck to a stop outside Sophia's apartment building, and again the *whoosh* of the airbrakes and *tick-tick* of the emergency lights through salsa music from the bodega in the center of the block.

The street is lively this warm night late in winter. Neighbors sit on stoops or fire escapes for the first time in a long time. Again the tailgate rises, the lift lowers, the log tied to the hand truck is wheeled down two steps as Sophia opens the storefront door, SHAPIRO'S CLOTHING in faint, flaking letters on the picture-window. She flips the light-switch, and after sputtering flashes the fluorescent lights overhead snap on brightly. There is an orderly chaos to her workshop, with a long wood table where chisels and mallets lay; tools hang on a pegboard; several framed canvases along the wall below two pictures torn from magazines taped to the brick; a bicycle in the corner. Half the cement floor is covered by a gray rug, painted-stained and frayed, and across the entire width of the studio in the back a paisley bedspread drapes nearly to the floor.

"Right in the middle," Sophia declares. The log freed from the hand truck seems even larger now than in the park.

"Something to drink?" she offers as Pete shakes his head with a grateful smile while rolling the hand truck outside. "Then something to read?" she calls after him and Terry encloses her in his arms; she briefly relents, they kiss once, then again more deeply.

On 1st Street a boy tries pulling down the truck's tailgate by the dangling strap while a bigger boy hops upon the running-board an instant before his mother shouts, "*Cisco, bajar de allí!*" from a stoop nearby.

"*Buenos Noches,* Señorita," an elderly man beside her calls to Sophia.

"*Buenos Noches,* Señor Rosario," she says as a young girl running by touches Sophia's elbow and Terry leans close for a quick kiss but she pulls away before he climbs into the truck.

"Thank you, Petie," she calls to him through the truck's open door.

Once at the wheel, after the *whoosh* from the emergency brakes released, Terry leans out the window. "So I'll see ya' around?" he says, eyebrows lifted hopefully as he jams the stick-shift in gear. She places a hand over her heart, then extends her hand to him just before the truck rumbles down the street and makes a wobbly left turn as Sophia steps lightly back to her store front.

"Sophia," Señor Rosario says sorrowfully from the stoop, "why don't you let that nice boy kiss you?"

She rolls her eyes while taking the two stairs down and back inside.

An hour later, her studio dark except for a candlestick in the center of the log, a delicate calico cat sniffs the new arrival as Eric Satie's *Gymnopèdies* spins on her record player. Sipping white wine and taking thin puffs from a thick joint, Sophia slowly trails her fingertips along the ridged, rough bark half-an-inch thick. She believes her scavenged treasure is a sacred oak, a tree that often topples in hard storms with roots rarely deep enough for its long, outstretched limbs. Her hand slowly passes across the sliced surface of what was once a giant, then she leans close to the candlelight and counts the rings but soon stops, asking, "Are you a hundred?"

To Satie's haunting piano music Sophia always envisions beautiful, naked bodies slowly dancing in summer fields. She settles with a resigned collapse into a ragged, stuffed armchair facing the log as Noel instantly, effortlessly, lands in her lap. Sophia imagines the woman she will free from within the tree though freeing only part of her from the tree that she's becoming. Many months will pass before this project is complete and Sophia is eager to begin work early next morning. And after the long day, the weed, the mysterious music, and the wine, she drifts to sleep; her head slowly lowers and she hears the tree's heartbeat, a dim, distant *ba boom . . . ba boom* repeatedly, always the same, slow pace, the soft heartbeat unvaried *ba boom . . . ba boom,* the darkness faintly filling with the life within the tree. Returning, groggy, Sophia rises with effort, Noel spilling to the floor, and the instant the tonearm is lifted and placed in the carriage where it hadn't returned, the heartbeat ceases.

∽

EARLY THE NEXT morning, Sophia begins hollowing out the log. The studio is bright from humming fluorescents, sunlight spread in long shafts through the studio's picture window with ⸱⸱'IHTO⸱⸱ ⸱'O⸱ HAH⸱ in faded, flaking letters on the glass.

Wearing a loose, pale blue T-shirt with the flag of Chicago on the front, in bib overalls, her short, dark hair beneath a Green Bay Packers ballcap, wearing goggles, she chips away at the smooth-sliced top of the log. The chisel digs a half inch into it with every strong strike of the mallet before she flicks the wood from the cutting edge, then strikes the butt of the chisel again; she thinks of the legend of a tree's soft groan with each blow from a hatchet. Except for a few sips of strong coffee and pausing to shake out her hands, she continues this for the next three hours, repeatedly, a rhythm to each strike and fleck of the woodchips, her eyes focused where the mallet must hit and imagining the woman within the log.

Sophia loves working, making something new from something else. A finished piece was merely a bonus, for it is the process she loves—the slippery firmness working with clay; the scratch of a charcoal pencil over a sketch page; the smell of paints squeezed from silver tubes; and this scent of the tree when she always thinks of her mother from whom she had learned the secrets of wood.

In her workshop in the barn Wenonah still chisels, carves, assembles, then hand-paints accurate miniature replicas of totem poles sold at local festivals and Wisconsin county fairs. At a souvenir stand along Route 70, the totem poles crowd beside beaded belts made in Japan. Recently she'd been commissioned for a twelve-foot pole honoring Wisconsin's 26th and 36th regiments and the Ojibwas that fought beside them in the Civil War.

Sophia pauses, shakes out her hands, smiles at Noel—a furry ball in a patch of sunlight on the cement floor—then looks at first one and the other photographs torn from magazines masking-taped to the wall. In Bernini's *Apollo and Daphne* the swift god's embrace nearly seizes the fleeing nymph already in transformation. Tree-bark covers her feet and up one leg, her fingers now twigs with leaves; Apollo is astonished. Taped beside it, a photo of a bronze, naked woman on tiptoe, arching slightly, her upraised hands sprouting leaves in Gertrude Vanderbilt Whitney's *Daphne*.

To Sophia, raised at the edge of a Wisconsin forest, carving a woman from a tree seems inevitable. Her father Sam and his older brother Joe own a newspaper in Milwaukee, and it was Sam who suspected that television's popularity in the 1950s meant people will soon only watch the news instead of reading it, so the Bauer brothers bought at a steal a five-hundred-acre farm along clear, cold Cranberry Lake in Eagle River two hundred miles north to create a summer camp for city boys.

With the help of laborers from the Luc du Flambeau Indian Reservation nearby, the grounds soon had two playfields, two canoes, two rowboats, a pen of ducks, one for goats, a beach along the lake which the next year had a wooden dock for fishing. There were sunfish, blue gills, and perch, though one day Sam hooked a muskie which terrified some boys who avoided swimming for the rest of the summer. The campers ate and slept in the farmhouse but after two successful seasons, cabins were built.

Rather than returning to Milwaukee at the end of the first season, Sam stayed through the winter caring for the animals and grounds. He never really liked the newspaper business despite a bachelor's degree in journalism from the university in Madison, and he found more pleasure among the horses, goats, and wooded acres. He had a comfortable relationship with the Native Americans who were grateful for the good wages, and though most people found Sam's penetrating blue eyes unsettling, the Ojibwas knew he looked hard at the world and liked that he spoke little. In time they gave him the goats and two old horses, plus bows and arrows for an archery range where occasionally young men from the reservation taught the ancient skill but refused payment for doing so.

At the celebration for the harvest he met a slender woman of surpassing beauty with dark eyes, long hair black as a moonless night, and who could mount a horse bareback. They married and, in time, had two boys as Camp Hiawatha—named from the Longfellow poem Sam loved— prospered in the coming years. Then Wenonah gave birth to the girl Sam had secretly wanted most so that he might see a reflection of Wenonah as a child at least briefly. The baby was named for his mother who died peacefully the year before.

Sophia was a slender, agile girl with dark hair inherited from her mother and challenging, light eyes from her father. She cared for the animals on the campgrounds and for an old pinto named Billy she rode only with a hackamore so that a bit never pressed against his large, grinding teeth. Despite hating to kill animals she skinned rabbits and gutted fish as well as her older brothers could, and at fifteen changed the tire on the pickup truck. In all seasons she sketched trees but especially in winter when branches most resemble fingers, and with strips of birchbark, stems, feathers, and pine needles she assembled exotic creatures released on windy afternoons when they came to life in their maiden flights.

Students in Eagle River's small school were various bloods and breeds plus a few blonde children of Nordic loggers going back generations, but Sophia was only a fair student bored by math which seemed incomprehensible, and biology that never mentioned the mystery in plants and animals. Owing to her father she loved books, often visiting the small library in the basement of City Hall on Division Street. In class the teacher read aloud from *The Iliad* of brave Hector's death and his body dragged three times around Troy, but the teacher couldn't answer Sophia's question why every Trojan warrior hadn't stood on the city's strong walls shooting arrows at Achilles. "Surely at least one would strike his ankle," she declared assuredly. Her mother offered her a portion of the barn for her own studio space, and the high school music and art teacher recommended Sophia for

Chicago's Art Institute which gave her a scholarship covering tuition and fees for her talents as well as to fill newly encouraged ethnicity quotas since her mother was full-blooded Ojibwa.

Sam would drive his daughter in the station wagon to Chicago early on a chilly morning late in August beneath the Moon When the Geese Shed Their Feathers which Wenonah knew was a blessing. They rode a hilly two-lane as the rising sun lit the meadows and farms, then Sam picked up the wide lanes of the interstate, his anxiety about his daughter living in the city growing steadily with each northern suburb they passed. He easily found Sheridan Road, then the four-story apartment building on Greenleaf with the one-bedroom which her uncle's friend, a Chicago real estate broker, had saved for her, the rooms just as Sophia had hoped. After carrying her few bags and boxes, Sam lingered in the small kitchen where in their farewell embrace Sophia laughed tenderly at the tears in her father's eyes.

She immediately loved Chicago despite living near a street named for the general who believed the only good Indian was a dead Indian. The constant variety of the city captivated her, a surprise down each street and around a corner, a provocative smile on the "L" train to or from classes. Lake Michigan only a block from her apartment soon became a kind of sanctuary where she swims from June to late September and strolls the shoreline in winter, Chicago's notorious weather untroubling compared to Eagle River which remains below freezing half the year.

Her classes in the stately, white-marble building guarded by bronze lions overlooking Michigan Avenue showed artists' works and methods she never imagined. and she learned to see familiar objects in new ways. She often wandered the Institute's fine, few galleries and liked the huge iron sculpture by Picasso in Daley Plaza, and Calder's fifty-foot orange *Flamingo* feeding off South Dearborn, and especially Miro's colorful forty-foot-tall *Miss Chicago* even before curling in the concavity of the figure's bell-shaped skirt during her first magic mushrooms trip.

But most other outdoor statues were Abraham Lincoln or Civil War generals, and she knew she must move now to New York City to expand her talents, though first returned home. She rode Billy through the woods fearing she may never again see the dear, old nag, and she made her father promise the pinto wouldn't become dog food. Sam could barely conceal his worry that his daughter would now live in New York—Chicago had been hard enough on him—and her mother, customarily unsentimental, gave her a golden feather to help find her way home.

∽

WHEN HER RIGHT arm finally doesn't stop aching and her left hand no longer can firmly grasp the chisel, Sophia puts down the tools, vigorously shakes out her hands, removes her goggles and runs her fingers through her hair free from the sweat-rimmed ballcap. With a cold, sweet sip of coffee left in the cup, she leaves the studio, passing through the paisley partition, the bathtub along the wall, her platform bed, the narrow stove, the refrigerator, then opens the back door into the warm, late morning with Noel scampering behind her, and drops into a lawn chair, in the yard, in the sunlight.

Three stories above, Señora Rosario attaches with wooden clothespins her family's clean, damp clothes to a line stretching to a tree at the edge of the small yard. She watches as Sophia smokes a cigarette, and even from the third floor can see the girl is tired.

"*Buenos dias*, Sophia," she calls as a colorful shirt fastened to the line by its shoulders crosses the yard.

Looking up to the window, Sophia squints into the sunlight. "*Buenos dias*, Señora."

"And how is First Street's most beautiful artist? Have you eaten?"

After a weak laugh, Sophia says, "Soon."

"That means no. I shall bring down something just as—" and soap bubbles drift from the second-floor window of the adjacent building, bubbles descending from the dark, open window before their silent pop. Through a squint Sophia sends a tired smile to the bubble-blower though with the sun in her eyes sees only Angi's silhouette.

Tossing her cigarette into an empty Bustelo coffee can, she returns to her studio, sweeps up the woodchips, then cleans each chisel and rinses her goggles in the small sink at one end of the bathtub. She steps out of her overalls and tugs off the T-shirt, and in the doorway to the yard shakes the woodchips and dust from her clothes—and to the old man walking along East Houston, the sight of her in underwear even through the chainlink fence will be a sweet recollection all day. She fills the tub and is grateful for hot water, adds bubble bath granules, steps from her panties, then eases into this brief luxury. An hour later she's at work at the Old Master's loft a few blocks uptown.

Soon after moving into the East 1st Street storefront with SHAPIRO'S CLOTHING in faded, flaking letters on the picture window, having spent nearly all fifteen one-hundred-dollar bills her parents had given her in a deerskin wallet, Sophia needed a job. Comfortable with her nakedness after a childhood spent swimming nude in cold Cranberry Lake, she found work posing for art classes at NYU nearby but quickly knew she must find something else; holding a pose inflexibly was maddening. She wondered if Gay Parée lofts had heat and were there electric fans in New York studios a century ago, then walked home that night troubled that she knew only one artist's model, the gifted, doomed Camille Claudel.

A few steps from her storefront Sophia barks like a dog near the trash cans to scare away the rats unafraid of people.

One night, an elderly, renowned artist who occasionally taught and lectured at the school offered to buy her dinner after class. Though failing to seduce her, Max Waters found Sophia intelligent and seemingly devoted to her artwork as well as very pretty; remembering wistfully his own youthful struggles and those people who helped along the way, he offered her a job.

"I need assistants, clean-up crews, gophers, someone who can stretch canvas," then added impatiently, "there's always something."

Sophia immediately enjoys the variety of tasks and Max's young staff—John, slender and serious and seemingly in charge of all operations;

Diane, sweet, busty, very sharp, and a former lover of Max; his assistants Kylie, blonde and plump, and tall, graceful David who rarely emerge from the studio and, behind Max's back, call him affectionately "the Old Master" who "we keep alive just to sign the paintings." All worked in a colossal loft an entire city-block long on the top floor of a six-story building with an industrial-grade elevator. There was a distant, dark bedroom, a very large living room where hung a few of Max's abstract-realistic paintings on the brick walls merging with a kitchen, and a vast studio from where drifted the perpetual smell of paint and turpentine. Sophia also liked the look of the handsome, sturdy young man who'd occasionally appear along with a young Black man with cornrows and a hand truck. They carefully, competently, roll the crated painting to, then down the freight elevator and anywhere for delivery—the city, the Hamptons, and once to Longboat Key, Florida, where Terry and Pete swam in the Gulf of Mexico, its warm water reminding Pete of his home in Jamaica while Terry kept thinking about that dark-haired woman with the light eyes in Waters' loft and how fine she looked in jeans and Western boots.

After a word from Max in the right ear, Sophia's most recent sculpture was displayed at the Sparrow Gallery in Soho. To her delight mixed with regret that the piece no longer belonged to her, someone purchased it, a two-foot-high feather of wood. The quill points up and the crushed barbs at the tip serve as its base as if the feather carrying all the bird's life, she had thought of it, has fallen to Earth, a gift from the sky. Her share from the sale of *Icarus* was twice what she makes in a month at Max's, and she was mentioned in the *Times* review of the exhibit.

And so having pounded the mallet on the chisel and into the log all morning, after Señora Rosario's plantains and tomatoes with rice and beans, then a bath before lavishly coating her hands and to her elbows with lotion, Sophia leans against Max's double kitchen sink, John near the refrigerator and Diane at the kitchen table spread with bagels and cream cheese, several jams, coffee cups and a carton of Sunkist Orange Juice, no pulp.

"And while the retrospective runs at Marlborough," John says, "we'll run a smaller show at the Parrish Gallery in Southampton for the summer getaways."

Sophia wonders if Max has any works of the Hamptons that the Parrish could display, and Diane remembers a watercolor of his two young daughters at the beach on Shinnecock Bay and several sketches of renown poets sitting around Max's pool in Southampton. Max emerges from the deep studio rubbing his hands with a soiled cloth smelling of turpentine; he nods distractedly at his staff and asks Diane, "Find those slides?"

"They're on the projector."

His dark hair with wide streaks of gray is disheveled, his intense eyes deeply set above a nose resembling a hawk's beak. He turns solemnly to Sophia. "Are you coming or what?"

"Yes," she sighs as if for the hundredth time.

To John he says invigorated, "Make sure the judges have enormous glasses to wear. Is Ginsberg back?"

"Still in Frisco."

"No one calls it Frisco," Max declares irritably.

John replies, "Otis Redding did," to which Max nods reluctantly and mutters, "True" just as David appears.

"Max," he says quietly, "you need to sign a canvas before we crate it," and Max follows him into the studio.

John says flatly to Sophia, "You know it's a costume party," and with a resigned smile she replies, "Of a New York statue."

Diane wonders if appearing naked counts as a costume.

"What statue is naked?" John asks.

"That one outside the Plaza Hotel," Diane says. "You know, she's holding a basket. Isn't she naked?"

Sophia tells her a basket should count as a costume.

"Fruit or something," Diane adds.

"She's Pomona," Sophia says, "Roman goddess of abundance."

Diane smiles at her with genuine admiration, then turns to John.

"Don't you just *hate* people who know about art?"

After work Sophia walks home down First Avenue in the soft evening when the city seems to take a breath after a vigorous day and before the mysterious night. Even more than Chicago she loves New York that only then was slowly emerging from dark decades of abuse and neglect, her neighborhood still ungentrified enough for struggling dreams to survive. There is an old Italian restaurant, a Jewish bakery, storefront markets of vegetables and fruits, narrow Indian restaurants with strings of colorful, miniature bulbs, the scent of coffee and butter cookies from Venierio's around the corner at East 11th Street, and though New York's pizza slices are better than Chicago's Sophia misses Chicago's Vienna hot dogs.

Sidewalks teem with pale teenagers dressed in black and safety pins, hardy Polish women in heavy coats and babushkas even on that warm evening, and pretty Puerto Rican mothers pushing carriages. Sophia still shops at the 24-hour Korean market despite the owner once chasing her away for sketching the outdoor displays of fruits and vegetables, and she loves that the slender woman taking the stairs down to the F train might dance at Lincoln Center that night, and the old man reading on a bench could be a famous poet, and *certainly* the Black man with the battered saxophone case is a musician here in this city of artists.

She turns right on East 1st Street, passing a small playground with a thin, tall spray of water, handball courts, and a paint-stained bedsheet on the sidewalk where a young man with tangled hair sells items—**A buck each** reads his cardboard sign. Sophia buys Cyndi Lauper's *She's So Unusual*, gazing while walking home at the LP's back cover with the bottoms of shoes from a Van Gogh painting and the derelict parachute jump at Coney Island.

A girl running by touches Sophia's arm.

"Jinny!" Sophia yells at her hurrying down the block.

Inside her storefront, Sophia lingers on the log though is disappointed at how little progress had been made despite hard hours that morning. Noel immediately meows faintly for food, and in the small living space behind the hanging, paisley bedspread she sees through her back window Señor Rosario bent over the metal doors leading to the basement. She places the grocery bag and her new, used record on the small table, takes an envelope from a small desk drawer and enters the backyard.

"*Buenos tardas*, Señor," she says, then calls down into the basement, "*buenos tardas*, Manny" a moment before "*buenos tardas*, Sophia" comes from the basement.

Señor Rosario straightens effortlessly before Sophia hands him the envelope.

"Sorry it's late as usual," she mutters with a small frown as he counts the cash, takes from his back pocket a receipt book, writes one, snaps it out and hands it to Sophia gazing into the basement.

"No hot water again?" she asks.

"Never buy anything a hundred years old."

"Not even a work of art?"

"That won't have a boiler," he says, then calls into the basement, "but Manny can fix anything."

"Anything," Manny, unseen, replies.

"You know," Señor Rosario says, then looks around suspiciously, leans closer and whispers, "there's a way to greatly lower your rent. If my wife is a problem," and he glances around again, "I can get rid of her."

Sophia, also whispering, "Bump her off, you mean?"

"In the movies they rub her out."

"But they always catch those guys, even in the movies."

Rosario smiles and leans back, no longer whispering. "But people love those stories. Dashing older Latin gentleman, beautiful young artist, passion, murder," and leaning closer, whispers, "I'll be acquitted, and more people will buy your artwork."

After several serious nods, Sophia replies, "Let me think about it."

She returns to her storefront as Rosario's desirous eyes following her soften to a smile.

Early the next morning, in bib overalls, the Packers ballcap, the goggles, with Cyndi Lauper on the turntable, Sophia is at work on the log.

*"After my picture fades*
*and darkness has turned to gray"*

With the mallet she repeatedly hits the chisel biting into the log, woodchips flying, her rhythm steady, her eyes focused on the butt of the chisel.

*"you can look and you will find me*
*Time after time*
*Time after time"*

# Chapter Three

Hosting the gala banquet for New York City's lavish celebration of itself was the Hotel Astor. Eleven stories, a thousand rooms: "*To have stayed at the Astor,*" read its advertisement, "*is to have lived in New York.*" A restrained exterior with a green-copper mansard roof in the Parisian style of the day, but such elegance and excess inside. Murals sensuous and heroic depicted the city's past. There was a Flemish smoking room, a billiard room patterned after Pompeii, an American Indian Grill with aboriginal artifacts from the Museum of Natural History, well-stocked bars of various notorieties and preferences, an underground wine cellar, and a roof garden the length of the hotel from 44th Street to 45th along Broadway. Almost within reach, soaring twenty-five stories, seeming to rise above the stars themselves, the magnificent Times Tower.

On the hotel's ninth floor, beneath sparkling chandeliers hanging from the vaulted ceiling of ivory and gold glittering in the mirrored walls and polished brass, the grand ballroom set for a premier banquet for five-hundred guests as if from a vision of Versailles.

"We gather tonight," declared the master of ceremonies over the murmurings of men in tuxedos, elaborate silk robes, generals with four-starred epaulets, the clergy's purple vestments, "to honor the deeds of the great explorer and of the inventive genius—" His voice carried above the fragile clink of saucers and glassware and the waiters' polished shoes to one balcony, and a second, then a third where women in colorful gowns gazed at the festivities below "—and celebrate the three-hundredth anniversary of Henry Hudson's discovery of this island at the edge of the New World."

Along the crowded, lively sidewalks of Times Square, Henry Hudson and Robert Fulton impersonators posed for flash powder photographs beneath banners

HUDSON-FULTON CELEBRATION<br>300 YEARS

like canvas rainbows above the streets.

"And merely a century ago when Robert Fulton's steam-powered boat *Clermont* forever ended the fickle tyranny of the wind."

Rumbling subways cross the East River Bridge—later known as the Brooklyn Bridge—as passengers gazed at the colossal granite towers above like an immense cathedral's arches a thousand years old; two-hundred feet below, freighters and sand scows and busy ferryboats churned the iron-colored waterways, and for twenty miles up the North River—soon renamed the Hudson River but *Muheakantuck* to the Native Lenape long before that—floated a great armada of schooners, lightboats, tramp steamers and paddle steamers, ocean liners, warships, and full-masted clippers with all flags and banners flying. Whistles tooted, bells clanged and clanged, foghorns blared. Leading the flotilla, an exact replica of Hudson's *Half Moon,* its jib and fore sail, main sail and gaffs billowing. Close behind, Fulton's *North River Steamboat*—some call it the *Clermont*—with its mizzen mast, jibs and spanker sail, black smoke curling from its smokestack rising to hot air balloons drifting above the shore lined with spectators dazzled and exuberant.

"But these coming weeks," the master of ceremonies assured the entitled gathering, "are tributes not only to the achievements of the past," and he nodded slowly, decidedly, a smirk growing to a boast, "but also to the glorious future in this city of limitless possibilities" and a few guests uttered "Hear Hear!" while others lightly applauded.

Fireboats on the Upper Bay shot waterspouts high above the sailboats and sloops, catboats and dinghies, and three times Wilbur Wright circled the head of The Statue of Liberty in his airplane made seemingly of toothpicks and paper, a sight so remarkable and transcendent, so hard to believe despite genuinely seeing, that even the eyes of the copper-colored Lady followed his flight.

"Oh Rozie," Audrey cried through a breath lost at the sight of it, "I must fly in one of those someday!"

"For this is a celebration of the spirit of New York City," declared the master of ceremonies, "a spirit that embodies a new century and the spirit of the modern world!"

New Yorkers by the thousands strolled the sidewalks in a kind of waltz, casual and enthralled, red lips and powdered cheeks, faces freshly shaven dabbed with Lilac Vegetal. Derbies and shirtwaists, a pushcart of flowers, pickpockets in snug vests, a pickle stand, bootblacks calling "Shine 'em up," a young peddler, black-bearded and stooped, pushing his rickety cart of baked sweet potatoes, and a tall man singing with his top hat at his feet upturned for coins:

*"Say hello to dear old Coney Isle, if there you chance to be,*
*When you're at the Waldorf have a 'smile' and charge it up to me—"*

"Never has a city grown so rapidly," the master of ceremonies declared, "so loftily, nor has overcome such difficult and particular challenges to not merely survive but triumph!"

Light applause and "Hear Hear."

"Merely a century ago this was a city of one-hundred thousand," he said, nodding several times before his voice rose, "and today," as he reached out to the audience, "it is a city of four and one-half million!"

American flags waved in the mild breeze from every shop and church, belltowers chiming above a great parade of elaborate floats both horse-drawn or mechanized. The *Half Moon*, followed again by the *North River Steamboat* amid spectators along the jammed sidewalks singing heartily—

*"Glory, Glory Hallelujah"*

as the 7th Regiment Marching Band played a rousing—
"*Glory, Glory Hallelujah*"
of "The Battle Hymn of the Republic" as all sang—
"*His truth is marching on.*"

"Fifth Avenue is as grand as any Paris boulevard," the master of ceremonies proclaimed. "Our mansions rival European chateaus. Here is the world's longest bridge, the tallest structures ever created—"

In a phaeton wheeling down Fifth Avenue, a young woman eagerly cried to her mother, "The Fuller Building really *does* look like an ocean liner sailing uptown."

"Well from *my* view," her mother replied, "it's a shape fit for an ironing board."

"—while under construction only blocks from here is the grandest train station the world has ever seen, its colonnade recalling the Roman Empire, here in the Empire City!"

All 3,671 velvet seats in Carnegie Hall filled to hear the New York Philharmonic perform Dvorak's symphony *From the New World*; sixteen blocks downtown on West 41st Street, Walter Whiteside playing David in Israel Zangwill's play *The Melting Pot* said "to think that all those weary, sea-tossed wanderers are feeling what *I* felt when America first stretched out her great mother-hand to *me*" at Collier's Comedy Theatre, its 625 seats sold out night after night.

At the corner newsstand on West 42nd Street, an article appeared with the headline,

## SECOND SMALL FIRE AT
## TRIANGLE SHIRTWAIST COMPANY

on page five of the *Daily News*.

"No one needs journey to Europe to hear foreign tongues," the master of ceremonies proclaimed, and his fingers tossed words like petals. "*Benvenuto, willkommen, dobro pozhalovat, bagrism*. We hear them every day on the sidewalks of New York. You ask, is there a place in the world where all nations can live in peace and harmony? *This* is such a place," he declared, "where the world arrives at our golden door in tens" and his voice rose impassioned, "nay hundreds of thousands yearning to breathe free—"

Lifted to Cooper Union's domed auditorium stage—the balcony jammed with tired-poor-angry workers—her young face still badly bruised from a policeman's nightstick but her dark eyes fiery, Clara Lemlich cried in Yiddish, "*Ikh bin a arbetn meydl,*" while beside her a sturdy man with side curls tucked behind his ears called out to the crowd, "I am a working girl." To her other side a woman with abundant hair yelled "*Sono una ragazza che lavora.*"

"—where in sunlit workshops downtown," the master of ceremonies proclaimed proudly, "those grateful, new arrivals find opportunity stitching the garments for the world."

Clara Lemlich gathered her strength to demand, "A*un ikh makh az mir nemen a general streyk*," and the woman beside her cried, "*e mi muovo che facciamo uno sciopero generale,*" and the man in black garments projected these words in challenge and defiance, "and I move that we go on a general strike," an instant before five hundred voices cheer like a declaration of war.

A million incandescent bulbs form glowing outlines on dignified City Hall, the Custom House, Washington Square's heroic arch, bulbs strung far uptown along slender, sloping Riverside Drive to Grant's great mausoleum encircled with lights. The million bulbs seemed to glow brighter as dusk turned to night when fireworks of red-white-blue splashed over the jubilant crowds, upturned eyes sparkling beneath—

HUDSON-FULTON

1609-1807

—in more incandescent bulbs crossing above crowded street corners where newsboys in news caps waved the latest editions—

**HOOPLA ON THE HUDSON**

**CITY BRIGHTER THAN BROADWAY**

—as coins jingled in their aprons.

For days those roaming the sidewalks had a swing, a step amid the scents of excessive perfume, flash-powder, horseshit, cigar smoke, and— near the cart of oysters a penny each— the sea. Taverns, restaurants, shops selling neckties, handkerchiefs, belts, bonnets, gloves, a cigar store with a life-size wooden Indian chief all opened for the excited throngs weaving past a sandwich board advertising QUEEN ELIZA and below that *Clairvoyant Extraordinaire.* The old gypsy woman sat delighted in a wicker chair, a lace capon on her head, wearing many necklaces, her eyelids heavy with shadow. Already she'd had several clients that festive night while trollies nudged their ways uptown and downtown among wobbly horse-drawn wagons, horse hooves clattering on cobblestone amid crowds in the street and on sidewalks and stoops, from fire escapes and open windows, then Queen Eliza's heart surged at the sight of Audrey whose gaiety dimmed when her eyes fastened on the old woman lost behind the tall black hats, waving scarves, and smoke.

Overhead in Central Park, along the docks and from the bridges, fireworks like luminous rain moments before tremendous explosions, New York giddy with joy of itself.

"Here on this little island," the master of ceremonies continued energetically, "the world has come with hope, with dreams, with indomitable desire—"

Standing on their tenement rooftop far downtown, watchful for fireworks' embers, each near a bucket of water, Jeremy Gavin and his nineteen-year-old son Gabriel gazed at midnight Manhattan illuminated, the Williamsburg Bridge outlined with incandescent bulbs as swooping cables glow while searchlights' beams waved like pale, luminous arms in the bright night sky pungent with gunpowder and crackling with the sound of fireworks.

"God said let there be light," Jeremy whispered turning to Gabriel whose face shimmered with light and then darkness and light again, "and it was good."

"—for the past three hundred years!"

The master of ceremonies raised his cocktail glass as did the five hundred guests at fifty tables.

"Tonight and for ten days we celebrate the past," then with his glass held high he proclaimed, "here in this city of the future!"

He sipped, then lifted first his eyes and then his champagne glass to the women elegantly gowned in the first balcony. Lifting his gaze and glass a touch more, to the women in the second balcony, and to those in the balcony above that, their jewels and dresses shimmering like the chandeliers above them. The women glanced haughtily, with a feigned, distracted curiosity, chatting contentedly among themselves while casting a shadowed eye on the festivities, and all aware of the many eyes turned upward from the men below. And with the women in the third balcony were three others far more lightly garmented, immobile, life-sized, and cut from a single block of marble, the *Three Graces*, the grand centerpiece specially commissioned for that glorious event. They are casually entwined, their white flesh pure and provocative, made so impossibly smooth not by sandpaper but surely with lotions from the gardens of Araby or the Encantadas. At the sight of them one felt a small leap of flame in the heart, a stirring of blood in the groin, an urge to touch if only to ascertain that it was cool marble and not warm flesh, and the longer one gazed the more that was imagined in this fantasy preserved in stone.

Three days before, while in Isidore Konti's studio, Audrey saw for the first time the finished piece for which she'd posed these last months.

"So beautiful," she said with hushed amazement.

"Their beauty is modeled after yours," Konti replied.

She was eighteen, fair, with long, dark hair and blue-gray eyes searching and bright, dressed simply in a crisp, white shirtwaist pinned at her wrists, a dark skirt below her knees, and dark shoes with a small heel.

"But beauty is only a portion of your gifts," Konti told her, then with an upturned hand indicated the watchful, protective figure lounging in the center. "Aglaea, for elegance." The thin garment covered all but her left shoulder, nipples aroused under the thin fabric of marble. "Her sister Euphrosyne," he said, "for mirth." His hand moved left to the figure swooning on her sister's shoulder, her gown having fallen beneath her breasts. The sister to Konti's right, "Thalia," her head resting lightly on Aglaea's hip, "for youthful beauty" though her face had a hint of melancholy, all her nakedness revealed to where the fabric gathered between her thighs.

"Each muse is different," Konti said, "and each endowed with the spirit *you* gave them."

Audrey felt a surging self-worth, not for her beauty, which she knew she had nothing to do with save taking care, but for her endurance, her freedom from modesty, and that she could find within her what Konti had asked.

"This centerpiece for the inaugural banquet of New York City's greatest celebration," he said to Audrey still gazing with pride and astonishment at the marble sisters, "also begins your debut, Miss Munson, as queen of the artists' studio."

And while gazing upon herself, her image preserved in three different auras, Audrey knew then that she'd forever exchanged her dream to be a Ziegfeld Girl for this that was not about herself but because of herself. She felt that she truly had left her girlhood aspirations behind now after finding something within herself she hadn't even known she possessed. *And to this*, she told herself, *I'll remain steadfast, devoting the fullness of myself to what may last a thousand years.*

∽

TO COMPLETE THE glorious New York Public Library on Fifth Avenue, the largest marble building ever created—**City Beautiful Turns The City Beautiful** ran a *New York Herald* headline for May 23, 1911—Frederick MacMonnies was commissioned to sculpt for the library's two exterior alcoves a nude male figure for one and a nude female for the other. First, he visited Konti at his studio searching for one in particular of the three models who had posed for *Three Graces*; the figure on the left, he said to Konti, "What was she, mirth?" That the same woman modeled for all three figures in the piece surprised the young sculptor who was now even more certain that she must pose for his *Beauty* to complement his *Truth* inspired by Keats' "Ode on a Grecian Urn" and ideal for the great library.

"Will she pose nude?" MacMoonies wondered.

Konti said to him, "Why not ask her."

For his memorial to Isidor and Ida Straus, Augustus Lukeman wanted his model lightly gowned and with perfectly proportioned ankles and feet, the reclining figure's toes dangling above a reflecting pool alluding to the cold waters in which the old couple had drowned on the *Titanic* the year before. Finding beautiful models was not difficult, but he wanted one with perfect ankles and feet; Audrey's were ideal, and with her hand contemplatively on her cheek, she held her pose while thinking of the wife given a seat on a lifeboat but refusing to leave her husband. Audrey believed this must be the most devoted of loves but wondered *would I have remained aboard had I been twenty-five instead of an old woman.*

Only Audrey's arms and hands initially interested Adolph Weinman recently commissioned by Queen Wilhelmina of the Netherlands for a restored *Venus de Milo*. With her hair tied high on her head, her torso bare and feeling a cool, quiet thrill because of it, with a chiton having fallen well below her waist, Audery resembled the ancient statue found only a century before. She rested her extended left arm on a pilar, the apple in her upturned hand given by young Paris of Troy in exchange for beautiful Helen. Audrey had lost earlier timidity since her light garment first fell before Konti's eyes. Now she often no longer only imagined herself as an image the sculptor was making tangible but as twenty-year old Audrey Munson, posing as the goddess of love for one of New York's most renowned sculptors. She held the pose just as Weinman wanted, and though his purpose was to sculpt only the arms, Audrey relished that his eyes also traveled slowly across her naked torso, and after seeing Audrey leave the Tenth Street Studio, Salvatore Scarpetti knew he had found the Lady Godiva he'd envisioned.

Except for the fakes of whom Rozie had warned—melancholy young men with only a sketch pad but an abundantly-pillowed velvet sofa, dark rugs on the floor, exotic lamps dimly lit, a hookah pipe, and a desire to see young women pose nude—Audrey found that artists' studios were similar; cold from November until sometimes into mid-April despite a wood-burning stove, and sweltering in summer. The lofts were large, some very large, with tall windows, a few with skylights and all with platforms and ladders and works in progress in clay or plaster, sometimes the same figure in various sizes on tables cluttered with mallets, chisels, measuring clippers, the air often hazy with plaster dust settling on everything, and on Audrey too after hours posing. But when each session ended, she rinsed, proudly knowing that all artists endure hardships in different ways.

Audrey's journey to work turned even more varied and exciting than those to the Lincoln Building when modeling at the Tenth Street Studios. The morning sun would rise over the hills of Upper Manhattan, always giving the city a glowing promise of possibilities; even gray skies had a thrilling, quiet power. She rode a streetcar down to 42nd Street where always Times Square stirred her with its endless, pandering variety of women in long, dark dresses, of men walking with surety and slender sticks. She imagined returning a glance and some brief, passionate embrace in a doorway before hurrying on.

She felt an eager rush of blood upon seeing the Hotel Astor and smiled in sweet recollection for what seemed long ago at the sight of the New Amsterdam Theatre on 42nd Street. *What would have come from that dream*, she wondered. *Would I now be a Ziegfeld Girl after all*, though having admitted before that her talents weren't exceptional. *But destiny*, and she smiled, *has a different plan for me.*

In a few minutes the swift, shimmying subway carried her to the West Fourth Street Station and the dense, narrow streets of Greenwich Village. There were aromatic Italian bakeries, men washing stoops, and mattresses draped over fire escape railings. In Washington Square she heard the whistling wings and the heartfelt coo of mourning doves as escorted children hurried to school. *Is the young man with wild hair a poet up early with inspiration or sleepless from heartache?* An old man in a floppy sunhat painted on a canvas the Arch beneath which passed somber, black motorcars, carriages pulled by fine horses, and a fragile, energetic penny-farthing.

Sometimes when she's leaving the Tenth Street Studios, a street nearby was in frenzy with clanging firetrucks pulled by powerful horses, their black eyes enormous as shouting men fought yet another fire in one of a hundred small sweatshops in the neighborhood. Late one early spring afternoon, Audrey hurried fearfully from the shouts, the alarm bells, and the smell of smoke.

Days later at the kitchen table, she sipped tea as Kittie glanced through the newspaper about yesterday's funeral procession despite the heavy downpour.

"The paper says the skies wept," Kittie read, then added, "Mostly Jews and Italians, it seems."

"Rozie's little sister worked in the Triangle Company," Audrey said, and Kittie turned to see her daughter's closed eyes. "But not on those top floors," Audrey whispered.

Kittie looked to the ceiling and crossed herself. "How her mother must be thankin' the Lord," then looked sternly at her daughter, "and *you* should be grateful you were born pretty."

"Oh Mommy, I think some of those girls were pretty too."

Long had Audrey known how her fine features and some bit of talent had kept her from the sweatshop's dark drudgery— the long, wearisome hours, the constant, nearly deafening whine of dozens of sewing machines in a cramped loft with splintered wood floors covered with cloth remnants and tissue scraps. But it was Kittie who stared fearfully at the newsprint wondering how she could ever survive without Audrey's success, then sent upward a silent prayer of thanks for her daughter's good fortune amid God's incomprehensible ways.

Returning home always seemed a longer journey for Audrey, especially in winter's early darkness with often a cold wind as she walked west from Broadway toward the wide, dark river. But their rooms were usually warm and always Kittie had the kettle on and a good dinner to follow. Audrey proudly dropped into her mother's hand four silver dollars one at a time but kept one for herself before collapsing into a kitchen chair with a tired, contented sigh.

"Another hard day?"

"Yes."

"And tomorrow?"

"Yes," Audrey smiled.

"Konti again?"

"Augustus Lukeman."

"Good," and she placed a saucer and cup on the table. "I don't trust Italians even though most of 'em being of our faith."

"Mr. Konti is Austrian."

"Or the Jews," Kittie added. "Do you need a rub tonight, my dear?"

The artists too were similar—many middle-aged, robust, with strong arms and shoulders, their hands very strong, each with facial hair in varied designs and places. Most were married with mistresses and all treated Audrey respectfully, doing nothing to jeopardize their relationship with the young Miss Munson regardless of her allure, for each knew what she gave to their work and used her as often and for as long as she was available.

For Attilio Piccirilli's larger-than-life women honoring the city's fallen firemen Audrey posed gowned and seated. For *Duty*, her arm encircled a young boy's waist, a fireman's helmet in her lap, her chin slightly lowered as she held a faint, anguished expression despite the boy's continual peeks—"Joey!" Piccirilli snapped again—down her loose garment.

For *Sacrifice*, Audrey's breasts were bared, her expression resigned, accepting, a dead fireman laying supine across her lap as she thought of the statue of Mother Mary with her dead son though of course Mary's breasts were covered. The muscular, young model now had his head tilted back, naked and pale to just below his waist where his heavy trousers sagged. Audrey was aroused by the sight and feel of him, by his strong arm limp behind her neck, and she wanted to stroke his upturned throat, along his muscular torso, her heartbeat quickening as she imagined her hand slipping into his heavy trousers, but she hurried this thought away. *I'm the fireman's widow now bravely accepting his death.*

So reliable, so comfortably compatible, her poses so haunting and held as if she were already stone, Audrey again posed for Piccirilli in three figures meant for the huge *Maine Monument* under construction at the southwest corner of Central Park. Most New Yorkers had already forgotten America's brief war with Spain little more than a decade earlier, but William Randolph Hearst wanted an entrance into the park grander than the entrance at the park's southeast corner financed by his rival Joseph Pulitzer. Here would be fountains and lounging, allegorical figures and a gowned woman standing upright in a boat, her arms extended, palms downward as if she bestowed a blessing on the city before her. Though having guided her pose, Piccirilli gave no direction to how each of Audrey's fingers differed in placement from the others and nearly unvaried; he was momentarily amazed and admired her for it. For the figure placed at the back of the forty-foot tower, her arms were again outstretched but with palms upward as if in offering, each finger again differing from the others.

Atop the monument's tower, a gilded goddess with a victory wreath raised high in her left hand, three golden, galloping horses reigned in with her right. Each night for a week Kittie massaged and placed Epsom salt compresses on Audrey's left shoulder, which would soon be raised again for weeks while holding the city's regal crown because Adolph Weinman was sure that Audrey Munson must be his model for the largest and most important statue on the island of Manhattan.

Forty-stories over the city on the new, Roman Empire-inspired Municipal Building—the center of city government and the last, great addition to "City Beautiful" by McKim, Mead and White—at the pinnacle 580-feet above One Centre Street, balancing on a great, gold ball above the colonnade and columns, she would radiate the Spirit Triumphant. Gowned, gilded, gleaming, the twenty-five-feet tall Civic Fame is visible across the city, and when the figure was complete and the scaffolding around it removed, the *New York Tribune* ran a front-page story with the headline, **DAUGHTER OF MANHATTAN'S HEAVENS BASKS IN ALL HER GLORY,** though the name of the statue was incorrect, Weinman's name misspelled, and the model never mentioned.

Also opened during this glorious time of construction in New York Pennsylvania Station— the most sublime structure the city had ever seen. Enormous colonnades extended two city blocks from 31st to 33rd streets along Seventh Avenue, with lofty, black-beamed waiting-rooms inspired by the ancient baths at Caracalla recalling distant empires only now here in the Empire City and built, declared *The New York Times*, to last for the ages. To parallel the huge, wreath-encircled clocks above the colossal entrances, Adolph Weinman created two eleven-foot-tall figures; Audrey was his model. For the endless comings and goings of the traveler, she wore a gown from neck to toes representing *Day*, her head uncovered, face uplifted; for *Night* she was downcast, her head shrouded, the garment having fallen down her body to just above the allure only inches lower.

Weinman was soon commissioned for a male and a female figure both later enlarged, with wings added to adorn outdoor fountains for San Francisco's 1915 Panama-Pacific Exposition. For *Rising Sun* he envisioned a nude male on tiptoes, arms and wings outstretched as the figure gazes upward with passionate greeting for the new day. His contrast and companion, *Descending Night*, would be a sensuous, nude female, also on tiptoes and with wings, and for this Weinman asked awkwardly that Audrey have no pubic hair, to which she quietly, without hesitation, agreed.

One morning Audrey stayed a while longer in a warm bath so that below her waist might soften even more. The tub drained of water, then she soaped her hands which she spread across her dark pubic hairs and between her thighs. She passed the safety razor over her there in slow, careful strokes, rinsed the blade beneath the faucet, then with one hand opened herself slightly and passed the razor there too. When the task was complete, her hand felt not the least stubble but only her softest parts as if she were still a young girl. She splashed warm water over her there, then lotioned herself there, quickly at first but soon feeling a pleasurable sensation as she moved her hand more slowly. The Sisters at Saint Francis Xavier had vehemently declared that a girl must never arouse herself in any way though one girl at the academy always found ways to move herself there against the corner of a table, and after a few more moments

Audrey quietly sighed to the soft waves of pleasure brought on by her fingertips across her smooth surfaces.

For *Descending Night* she posed standing, all of her revealed like the young Austrian soldier had done. Again her face was downcast as she had once posed for Weinman's *Night* on the great train station's clock. For that work, a garment had covered her below her waist, but now she posed naked as she had in her bedroom while reaching for the magic city out her black window a few years before.

For this piece her right knee turned modestly inward, her arms upraised holding back her hair. She held in her stomach so her ribs were visible, her left hip tilted provocatively a touch higher, and standing on tiptoes accentuated her perfect feet and calves. Though momentarily embarrassed in her nakedness, Audrey was also thrilled, as if she'd taken a breath of cool air. Weinman's final creation was more slender than Audrey's actual figure, and while he could have found a model who matched his final version of the piece, it was Audrey's remarkable ability to capture in every part of her pose the aura that Weinman sought. For *Descending Night* she had found within what she believed a nearly divine disposition and a contrast to the exuberance of dawn, something all hope for in sleep—repose.

"I've never worked with a finer model," Weinman said to Daniel Chester French over dinner at Polly Hollady's intimate basement restaurant on MacDougal Street in Greenwich Village. "She's beautiful and well-proportioned, of course," then, mildly amazed, "and untiring."

He wiped with a napkin first his mustache and then the corners of his mouth, adding, "But more than that she has an uncanny ability to feel what I intend. I say do this," and his uplifted hand opened, "and she makes it better. She's not only a model but a collaborator," then shook his head in mild bafflement. "Quite extraordinary. And at times she emits an aura during a pose that Renaissance painters would use as Madonna or Rembrandt for a portrait."

Weinman leaned forward. "Daniel, perhaps she will end your search in that piece you've been struggling with all this time."

AUDREY CLEARED THE dishes in their new apartment on West 77th Street with its two bedrooms and larger kitchen and their own facilities, even with a bathtub. They were closer now to the center of things, with good money coming in, much better than the chorus line though occasionally Audrey wondered wistfully where that might have led. She *had* loved performing on stage and the eager, happy applause that followed but knew she was on a destined path now and had absolute faith in the power guiding her. Besides, never had she seen her mother so happy. "You're going to make us famous," Kittie declared.

On some mild days Audrey would walk to the Lincoln Arcade Studio and home again, enthralled with the stores along Broadway—a French florist, the Italian markets, the Jewish bakery, Irish pubs, a Chinese laundry. The city was like the tapestry in the museum only with aromas and people and noise rather than the many colors of the wool. Often, she caught the smile and eager eye of a man she passed, then laughed to herself at what he'd think if he knew she posed naked only a little while ago. *Would he be angry, thrilled, and would he want to watch?*

But all that night Audrey had been quiet, and Kittie knew fatigue was not why.

"And what besides your aching body troubles you tonight?"

With a weak laugh, Audrey said, "How you know me," and settled in a chair at the table.

Kittie poured tea while declaring, "Bein' that you're me only child I should think so," then perched on the edge of the chair across from her. "Now what's so heavy on your heart?"

After a long moment, Audrey spoke calmly, seriously.

"This piece by Mr. French, a woman holding a mirror tilted so she's looking behind her."

Kittie waited, then said, "Watchin' her back as they say."

Again Kittie waited though Audrey only sighed wearily.

"So why is this so troublin'?" Kittie asked. A crease deepened between Audrey's eyes, then, more animated, she uttered slowly, "He calls it Memory, and I think the woman is looking at her past. Maybe remembering when she was prettier, certainly younger."

Kittie waited for her to go on. "And it's this what's troublin' you?"

"This woman is looking at her past," and Audrey lifted her eyes to her mother, "but I'm looking at my *future*."

"B-god child," Kittie cried with a baffled laugh, "what are you sayin'?"

Audrey stirred her teacup with a small spoon as the familiar, heavy mood descended on her again as it did each time she took that pose. When posing she'd always felt heroic, pensive, hallowed, enchanted. But this piece—and she spoke again, her voice soft and thoughtful.

"It's like something Gabriel read to me, that nothing can bring back the glory of the flower."

Audrey continued stirring the tea, the spoon softly scrapping along the cup.

"What is behind her is coming for me too," she cried with quiet, rising urgency. "Not next month or next year but ten years from now. I'll never again be as pretty as—"

"You'll *always* be pretty," her mother declared.

"I know," Audrey said, struggling to make all this clearer. "But there comes a day—"

"There comes a day you shouldn't be worryin' about today," Kittie interrupted. "Besides, we all grow older unless we die young and you don't be wantin' that," as she quickly crossed herself and looked up for an instant, "now would you?"

Audrey smiled with effort and sipped her tea, but again a thin crease deepened between her eyes.

"Sometimes I think of what that fortune teller said when I was a girl."

Kittie, exaggerating her shock, cried, "That awful *gypsy* woman?"

"Queen Eliza," Audrey whispered.

"That was a *carnival* show," Kittie cried through a forced laugh. "She can't tell the *future*!"

"She said I'd be famous," and worry filled her eyes. "She's right about *that*."

"And that you'll be wantin' for a penny," Kittie said defiantly, "yet we're doin' rather well I'd say."

Kittie settled herself with a quick, hard nod and a deep breath.

"Only a bit ago you were a little nobody in a chorus line and today there be statues of you all over New York," but her anger briefly returned. "So *there* you old gypsy queen."

Audrey's distress faded with a soft laugh at her mother's temper—Mama Bear protecting her cub—and after tea, a bath, after dabbing milk on her face and her mother's good-night kiss on her forehead, her troubled heart had eased. But that night Kittie slept restlessly, worrying what would come of her when those days Audrey feared at last, inevitably, arrived.

∽

THE NEXT MORNING—a damp, cloudy morning early in August, a dull sky barely brightening to the east—after catching the subway at West 72nd Street that rattled her to the West Fourth Street Station, Audrey hurried to the gated entrance of MacDougal Alley. Once inside, she passed rows of two-story houses along each side of the cobblestone roadway with a few carriage houses and a stable among the art studios, the sweet equine scent mixing with the smells of oil paint and plaster dust. She entered French's studio, his assistants already at work, and in a dressing room removed all her clothes before covering herself with a robe that felt heavy this warm, muggy morning.

In the studio Audrey and French exchanged silent nods, he occupied with his tools for the work ahead. She sat on a chair without arms, and after setting her resolve that she was an image in the mind of the sculptor—only that, something that isn't yet real—she removed the robe that draped across the chair and fell to the floor. A young man handed her a small mirror while glancing rapidly once along her naked body.

"Thank you," she said without raising her eyes to him.

Taking the pose that took days for French to discover—sketch-paper tossed to the plaster-dust-covered floor—Audrey reclined, her body turned slightly for her left leg to raise a little, her right foot resting behind her left ankle. She placed her left hand on her left thigh, the tilted mirror reflecting a wooden scaffold and a dark wall behind her, and soon—and sooner each time she took this pose— her spirit dimmed but she remained steadfast.

French worked swiftly as the image he sought took its vague rendering, Audrey motionless, barely breathing. For now his eyes mostly focused on the tablet as he switched from black chalk to gray, and while the morning passed slowly for Audrey—her gaze fixed on the mirror, the scaffold, the dark wall and her future—French repeatedly snapped glances at her, then back to the paper, rubbing the image with his fingertip, looking at Audrey again but at her face which to his momentary astonishment was quietly resigned, a little mournful, then he ceased sketching.

Well he knew of Audrey Munson's renowned, uncanny way of embodying the mood of a piece with each pose, but as his eyes remained fixed on her face, he felt a surge of doubt rush upward to his throat: *Where in that face in that mood? Her downcast eyes? The faintest turn of her lips?* And though he knew this must be the expression for the sculpture, he was uncertain at his ability to capture it in stone.

# Chapter Four

On Saturday afternoon after three days of miserable heat that broke the night before with a hard rain, Sophia rides to Terry's apartment uptown on her bike that has thin tires, five gears, and upright handlebars with handbrakes; she calls it Billy. In jeans, her light blouse billowing, and—since watching *Rocky* on a VHS as a child with her brothers in the paneled den—black Converse All-Stars, she takes First Avenue up to East 60th Street, then west to Central Park.

The rain had cleaned the streets and revitalized the park's trees. She rides slowly beside a horse pulling a carriage, watches its strong, shifting thigh and listening to the rhythmic *clop…clop* of its iron-shoed hoofs. She follows the winding roadway, then down the Great Hill, leaves the park at Strangers' Gate and heads west along 106th Street to Terry's apartment on West End Avenue. He buzzes her in as she shoulders her bike and climbs the two flights though once he had come down to help but received a glare from the sternest eyes he'd ever seen. At his apartment door he leans for a kiss but then she quickly withdraws. "I'm all sweaty." After showering she takes from her backpack a summer dress, fresh panties, and moccasins.

Terry would rather stay in bed with her all evening, but they leave for the Metropolitan Museum of Art knowing she'll return with him afterwards.

He convinces the young taxi driver to take them to Fifth Avenue and 86th Street "off the meter for a five." Having chiseled at the tree all morning and with two months' hard work behind her, Sophia is certain she'll not feel what she often does when visiting this, her favorite museum, that she should be in her studio working. But this late afternoon is a holiday.

To Sophia the building resembles a grand palace with arches and columns stretching along Fifth Avenue, the great lobby with its high ceiling, urns filled with lush bouquets, and cool, stone passageways. She takes her time floating through the galleries with their white walls where paintings hang and visitors linger, silent and enthralled. On one large canvas, lush, naked Venus in her futile attempt to keep young Adonis from his fated hunt, and Sophia recalls the soft hours when her father read to her from the large book of Bulfinch's myths of Greece and Rome. The book was abundant with photographs of the legends depicted in paintings and sculptures by great artists, and with her head on his shoulder she'd gaze dreamily on the pictures as Sam read the stories in a voice barely above a whisper.

In a tattered Metropolitan Museum guidebook she had found at Max's loft a small picture of Théodore Chassériau's painting *Apollo and Daphne* which Sophia quickly spots in its ornate frame across the gallery. Apollo is on his knees, his arms enclosing Daphne's pale nakedness, "But only here is the transformation," Sophia whispers, her fingertips nearly touching the emerging tree trunk on her legs, her arms upward reaching, as do Apollo's as if in worship.

With the task complete, Sophia strolls with Terry through the American Wing, past contemplative Hiawatha, sleek, golden Diana, and a bronze mountain lion with her cubs, the sculptor's name vaguely familiar to her—*Kemeys*, she says to herself, *Kemeys*. Terry bends his right leg that takes most of his weight while his arms imitate *Hercules the Archer*; beside him Bourdelle's muscular, bronze, life-size nude crouches, their eyes intent on where the arrows soar. Sophia feels a small thrill rise in her at the figure's nakedness, his muscular torso and powerful legs, his thick, flaccid penis along his thigh, and before their fingers entwine, she brushes the back of her hand across the zipper of Terry's linen pants.

Beside a seated, reclining, life-size nude woman in white marble on a pedestal, Sophia leans back, extends her left arm and gazes at an imaginary mirror in her hand.

"No," Terry insists, "she's looking behind herself."

Sophia drops the pose. "Be*hind* her?" and looks again at the sculpture.

"Like at her past," he adds.

She reads the word "Memory" chiseled in the pedestal.

The beautiful figure is milk-white, smooth as lotion, and yes, the mirror tilts not to herself but behind her. Sophia drawing so near to it elicits a stern "Please not so close" from the pouting guard to whom she smiles apologetically, then as close as allowed she gazes on the face with its strong jawline, its full cheeks, at the bridge of its nose, the heavy eyelids smooth and white like the sacred Miigis seashells her mother keeps in a small basket—and the statue's tender expression, reflective and faintly mournful.

Sophia is quiet when they leave the museum and enter the humid night; Terry lets her be. Perhaps she's thinking of what she'd seen in the museum or else of her own work, and she may even wish she were in her studio now though Terry doesn't offer since he wants her in his bed. And after another "five off the meter" the taxi leaves them at Broadway and 106th only steps from his apartment. They walk through the narrow, block-long Straus Park where Sophia lingers on the bronze statue of a reclining woman lightly gowned, her sandaled foot dangling just above the basin where water trickles. She passes her hand across the figure's hand, then along the cheek, stroking gently.

"Not so close, please," Terry says.

"How lucky we can do this," Sophia says dreamily. "Run our hands over her body, look closely into her eyes." After gazing on the figure's face for a long moment, Sophia wonders, "Who were these women who posed? What became of them?" Her fingertips trail along the name AUGUSTUS LUKEMAN carved in the bronze. "We know the sculptors, but who was their model?"

Terry knows the question was directed to the Universe but replies, "The face of The Statue of Liberty is Bartholdi's mother."

Sophia gazes on the figure's profile, drawing closer, only inches away, and then—as Terry has seen when she's amazed—her lips slightly part.

"What?" he asks.

Sophia withdraws slightly as her focus intensifies on the figure's heavy lids like bronze, smooth seashells, the full cheeks, its profile, then shakes her head and whispers, "I don't know" while stepping from the basin where Terry's hand gives balance. She presses against him, and he sways with her while singing poorly.

> *"Ain't it wonderful to be*
> *Where I've always wanted to be"*

Sophia moves gently in his embrace.

> *"For the first time, I'll breathe free*
> *here in New York City"*

She looks up into his eyes. "Let's to bed."

Terry is a patient lover despite his quick arousal which Sophia finds curious and a source of mild wonder at his desire for her. He always puts her pleasure before his own except one summer night on her roof, her back to him, her skirt lifted as she held the retaining wall, her own passion heightened at knowing the immense pleasure he was taking from her.

That night in his bed her waves break against him with her soft cries, her breathless release as she clings to him. Afterward, he says nothing once his breath returns, certainly not, "I love you," which he does but had agreed never again to mention. He rouses himself slightly and she sees his sly, satisfied smile and knows he loves her; after such pleasures, she even loves him.

When he rolls off her to his back Sophia takes a small swallow of sparkling wine from a glass on the bedstand, and then another sip which she sends in a cool stream through his lips. By now they've both returned from where their pleasures had taken them, so in the dark, simple room with the large brass bedframe, she reads to him by candlelight about the woman who becomes the tree.

" 'At once Apollo loved her,' " she recites, " 'and she at once fled the name of love. But a god can run more swiftly.' " She shifts a little while returning the fallen sheet to her bare shoulder. " 'Then seeing the river that is her father cries 'Help me, divine father, change this body that has given too much delight.' "

Sophia stops, displeased.

"See," Terry says. "It's not the *guy's* fault."

After an aggressive breath she continues reading; Daphne's limbs grow heavy, breasts enclosed with bark, arms now branches, her " 'once swift feet rooted and held.' "

Sophia lifts her eyes to his. "Now listen to this," then returns to Ovid. " 'And Apollo placed his hand where he had hoped and felt the heart still beating under the bark.' "

She remains looking at the page, his eyes on her shoulder and down to her small breast from where the bedsheet again had fallen.

She looks up, then, irritated. "Were you listening?"

His hand slips into the warm folds of the sheet to her thigh. "And placed his hand where he had hoped."

"No," and she folds her knees together while rolling to her side, "not again."

"Spend the night," and his arms enclose her hips.

"I want to work in the morning," as she weakly wrestles in his embrace.

"I thought *real* artists smoke opium and sleep until two."

She no longer resists but looks at him firmly. "Those were French poets, and if you *must* know I'm here only for great sex and your shower" and pulls him closer. "You *always* have hot water and such nice body wash," then she rolls on top of him and covers them both with the bedsheet. "And your *towels!*"

⁓

EARLY MORNING IS warm and gray and feels as if more rain is coming, the New York sky thinly overcast and dull. Sophia rides a block west on

106th to the service road of Riverside Drive from where she can see the great river rippled and solemn and dark rolling at ebb tide to the sea. Gliding downtown against the one-way traffic, graceful buildings to her left, Riverside Park to the other side, she hears the soft calls of mourning doves, their whistling wings when they fly. From a car at the stop-sign, "Hey sexy," he says through his open window, "you're going the wrong way." Knowing he watches in his rearview mirror as she rides, she rises off the seat and arches slightly.

At 100th Street she glances upward at a large memorial on the right with a seated woman, bigger-than-life, staring straight ahead and uptown, her granite profile sharp against the gray sky. Sophia flinches, slows, then loops back for another look at the profile, at the figure of a man, supine, across her lap, and again at the profile and the bridge of its nose. Sophia wheels her bicycle to the other end of the large sarcophagus dedicated, reads the inscription across it, to New York firemen, and finds another figure of a woman facing downtown, her chin slightly lowered, a fireman's helmet in her lap, her arm encircling the waist of a young boy beside her. Sophia is certain the profile is the same as the other woman, then her heartbeat surges. She mounts her bike and races back to the little park a few blocks away, to the gowned, reclining woman with the trickling water beneath her sandaled foot. The bridge of her nose; her full cheeks; that jawline; her eyelids like smooth seashells.

Back at the memorial to firemen, Sophia reads in the chiseled stone of its wide pedestal ARTILIO PICCIRILLI SCULPTOR. She looks at the figure's face awhile, and then at the other figure's face and believes one woman posed for all three sculptures, and perhaps *Memory* from the night before. To the pensive figure holding the boy, Sophia asks, "Do I *know* you?"

∽

AFTER ANOTHER WEEK with chisel and mallet—the log hollowed out enough for a vague torso emerging within it—Sophia finishes a little early, bathes grateful for the hot water, and after applying much skin lotion to her hands and arms she dresses in a plaid flannel shirt, her jeans, and the Converse All-Stars before biking up First Avenue, then cutting across East 40th Street to the library on Fifth Avenue. On the terrace she locks her bike to a green, metal chair near a statue within an alcove of the white, marble building. A figure of a pale woman, nude, leans slightly back against a white horse, her gaze and right arm uplifted. Sophia likes the figure's mild distress, her full hips and thighs, and the white horse. She wonders who modeled for this, and who modeled for them all. Not those of famous men but, for a start, the model she's been seeing uptown.

Slowly she strolls beneath marble arches and enters the vaulted ceiling of Astor Hall, then up the grand staircase to the McGraw Rotunda where Edward Lanning's four, tall murals tell the story of the written word. Above her, Prometheus steals fire from the clouds.

At a long, wooden counter a young librarian with a scruffy beard at a computer asks quietly though his eyes remain on the screen, "How, fair lady, may I be of service?"

"I need a book on New York statues," she tells him, nearly mentioning her search for a certain model's name but nothing about possibilities for a costume party.

"City or state?" he asks the computer.

"Screen," she tells him.

Momentary puzzled, he laughs and finally looks at her.

"Sorry," he apologizes, mildly embarrassed. "It's catnip."

"I knew you were just under a spell," she tells him, then, "Try city."

He returns to the computer and soon finds three choices. Sophia leaves with one, and that night in bed sipping chilled white wine—Noel in the dark studio slapping repeatedly at the dustpan banging across the concrete floor—Sophia gazes at the glossy cover of *All Around the Town: A Walking Guide to Outdoor Sculpture in New York*. It is a close-up color photograph of a gowned, golden woman at the pinnacle of a building high above the city, a crown uplifted in her left hand. Sophia slowly turns the pages of the large, slender book with its fine photographs of The Statue of Liberty, the angel in Central Park, General Sherman gold and heroic, Joan of Arc on horseback, her arm and visor raised as Sophia feels a hot flash of brief rage for what men do to women, then wonders if Joan had felt abandoned by God. There is a photograph of coy *Pomona* at the Pulitzer Fountain, a Native American and his dog, and regal *Miss Brooklyn* and *Miss Manhattan*, both large, grand, enthroned; words below the photographs tell how 'Robert Moses had the statues moved from the Manhattan Bridge to the terrace of the Brooklyn Art Museum because they impeded traffic flow' and that they were created 'by Daniel Chester French.'

After a moment, she whispers, "Memory." She looks hard at the photographs which are too small to tell if these faces are the face of the model of the woman with the mirror looking at what's behind her. The next day she travels to see these statues on the museum terrace but only after Angi—naked on her knees facing Sophia's wall with her hands on it for support—poses for sketches, each page tossed to the paint-stained rug.

"*Dios mio* this is hard," Angi says, aching and exhausted.

Another sketch falls to the floor.

"My knees hurt," Angi moans, shifting her weight. "How much longer?"

Sophia sketches quickly, her eyes intense on Angi's torso, along her slightly arched back to her waist.

"An artist's model poses for hours," she replies. "You haven't posed fifteen minutes," then lifts her eyes to her, "and stop *moving* so much."

Angi has a curved, vigorous body, her flesh the color of tupelo honey. The focus of Sophia's sketches tapers to Angi's waist before rounding to her bottom which Angi feels is perfect for a Latina.

"What do models think about for all that time?" she asks. "Is somebody playing flute or reciting erotic poems?"

Sophia continues sketching, changing angles and views, now capturing the slight upward swoop of Angi's right breast.

"At least you get to look on my nice *culo*."

"A very nice *culo*," Sophia says undistracted.

"Why from the back?"

After a moment, "More mysterious," she says and changes angles again, "and less complicated."

Angi takes a deep breath while shifting uncomfortably.

"And this girl turning into a tree. What's that about?"

Focused, unemotional, Sophia replies, "She doesn't want to get raped."

This startles Angi; she shakes her head, discouraged.

"Fucking men," she mutters.

She broods for some minutes, shakes her head again to clear the anger, then says, "Put on some music."

"What do you want to hear?"

"That cassette of Roberto Carlos."

Sophia's concentration weakens though she keeps sketching.

"I can't work while listening to Roberto Carlos."

"Because you'll think about Zihuantanejo with Estabon," she teases as Sophia slams the pencil to the tablet.

"You are the *worst* model. And stop *talk*ing I can't concentrate."

She picks up the pencil and returns to sketching.

Angi facing the wall emits a small, bored sigh. "Can't you do two things at once?"

"Angi!"

Angi takes an exasperated breath.

"And stop *moving* so much!"

Only after a few moments, Angi mutters loudly, "*Dios mio* this is hard."

Despite Angi's difficulties and distractions, Sophia has captured some of what she needs. Angi dresses quickly and the two ride a graffiti-ravaged, rumbling D train to the Brooklyn Museum of Art.

"Why Brooklyn?" Angi asks. "Not enough statues in Manhattan?"

"There's one called Miss Manhattan. Maybe I'll be her for Max's party," then adds, "and I must get a close look at her. Miss Brooklyn too."

The subway emerges from the tunnel when crossing the river on the Manhattan Bridge as Sophia changes her seat to the other side of the car to better see the mighty Brooklyn Bridge over the dark river below.

"You already Miss Manhattan," Angi says. "You're from somewhere else, you're beautiful and love the city. Us natives hate it," and she shakes her head and laughs, "but you immigrants still think it's the promised land."

Flattered and pleased, Sophia nods thankfully to Angi's bemused smile.

The subway again descends underground.

"What time is rehearsal?" Sophia asks.

"No rehearsal," Angi replies flatly. "We all quit."

"The whole cast?"

"All of us, *todos*," then she says, annoyed, "It's a play by Federico Garcia Lorca and the director casts an *Ital*ian girl for the lead."

Shaking her head, sympathetic, Sophia says, "That's America," and after a moment adds, "Didn't Natalie Wood play Maria in West Side Story?"

Even the warm blast of air that hits them as they climb the littered stairs to Eastern Parkway is relief from the stifling subway platform that remains hot until October. They cross the busy parkway to the great, sprawling museum where at each end of its semi-circular terrace is an enthroned woman in stone, twelve-feet tall, heavy-gowned, laurel wreaths in their hair. Sophia hurries to one of them. The figure is proud, regal, a peacock beside her, her fist perched on her thigh, elbow pointing outward defiantly.

"Miss Manhattan," Sophia declares with certainty, though with its chin slightly lifted she's unsure if this is the woman of her search, and the statue is placed in a way making it impossible for her to get closer. She wonders who had the idea of the fist, the sculptor or the model.

At the other end of the terrace is another statue, this one majestic too but modest, chin lowered, with a child reading at its feet. "Miss Brooklyn," Sophia says to the female figure. Even from the terrace Sophia feels certain the same woman posed for both of these and perhaps modeled for *Memory*.

"That's you too, isn't it?" she asks the stone profile.

"Who?" Angi wonders vaguely.

"I don't know," Sophia mutters, her eyes lingering on the face, then asks the figure, "Who *are* you?"

At the Blue Heron Café on Sterling Street, sitting across from Angi at a small table near the window, Sophia is eager and troubled, the afternoon sun through the lace curtains throwing a wavy, flower-pattern across her face.

"Daniel Chester French did those two statues," she says to Angi, "and I think he used the same model for Memory at the Met." Leaning closer she adds less assuredly, "And maybe she's the women on that firemen's memorial on Riverside Drive, and the one in that little park near Terry's."

She stirs her coffee, the dainty spoon softly scrapping in the glass cup, then shakes her head, concerned. "Who *was* this woman who's all over town, this Miss Manhattan?"

After looking a while at her troubled friend, Angi dips a fingertip into the small pitcher of milk and whispers, "Why don't you find out," then very lightly places a drop above Sophia's lip, rubbing softly, then another drop in tender circles on her cheeks. The two smile into each other's eyes.

∽

ON THE NEXT Friday after work, Sophia returns to the Metropolitan Museum open until nine that night to be sure the face of these women she's seeing throughout the city is the one who posed for *Memory*. Later she'll arrive at Terry's with his fresh sheets, sparkling wine, and desire, but for now she enjoys her solitary stroll through the quiet galleries, passing cases of ancient artifacts, portraits in elaborate frames of people from ages ago, a still-life of a bouquet with petals that never wilt since art defies the ephemeral. In the American gallery with the wall of windows to a darkening Central Park, she looks at *Memory* hard and long, intentionally doubting what she sees as the Art Institute had taught her so that she might look with new eyes; she is certain the model is the same, nods once assuredly, but while leaving the gallery she glances to her right where mounted on the wall is a statue of a woman larger than life, gowned, an arm holding back a hood shrouding her head. After only a moment Sophia believes the figure's face resembles all the others she's been seeing, then she shakes her head, discouraged. *Will they all now look like her?* She reads the plaque *Mourning Victory* and her heart surges—Daniel Chester French.

∽

SOPHIA ENJOYS THE Old Master's costume party and reproaches herself for her earlier begrudging attitude. The fluorescent lights are off, and table lamps turned low, with many crisscrossing strings overhead of little lights inside plastic red and green peppers and white skulls. Everyone is in costume as if a fragment of the Greenwich Village Halloween Parade from the week before somehow wandered to East 13th Street, took the freight elevator to the top floor, and ended up in Max Waters' loft. The soulful trumpet of Miles Davis blows from a tape deck on a window ledge and drifts among the casual conversations and over the kitchen counters with their platters of pastrami and corned beef sandwiches on rye, kosher pickles, plastic containers of cole slaw, and greasy bags of French fries beside cans of Dr. Brown sodas from the Second Avenue Deli. Behind a table and dressed as Alice in Wonderland, Angi serves drinks.

"Because of magic mushrooms and hookah-smoking caterpillars?" Sophia asks.

"Alice was my first leading role," Angi declares, then with a light, baffled voice, " 'I've often seen a cat without a grin but a grin without a cat is a most curious thing.' "

Instantly herself again, she asks Sophia, "So whatcha drinkin'?"

"You decide."

Beneath the table, an ice bucket from which Angi takes a bottle of champagne. "This is the good stuff," she whispers conspiratorially.

Someone bare chested and dressed as a Native American drags a large, stuffed dog. Max's assistant, David—a Civil War soldier in a kepi and holding a toy musket—weaves through the guests snapping pictures with a polaroid camera. John looks strikingly like Elvis with his hair slicked back and carrying a guitar even though there is no statue of Elvis in New York City. "There should be," he replies haughtily. Diane holding a basket really *is* nude beneath her bathrobe, and the Old Master in a green blanket, a green foam rubber crown, his face green, a red plastic handbag in his left hand held close to his chest, in his right hand an enormous rubber cigar uplifted, asks, "Guess who I am."

After a puzzled moment, Sophia says, "I give up."

"And who are you?" John asks her.

Wrapped in her only other bedsheet tied at the waist, her arms exposed, a bra on the outside, plastic garlands in her hair and holding a cantaloupe instead of a globe, she lifts her chin, puts her fist on her hip, elbow pointing out, and says proudly, "Miss Manhattan!"

John, Diane, and the Old Master stare at her blankly.

"Who's Miss Manhattan?" Max wonders.

Sophia drops her pose. "Who's Miss Man*hattan*?" she asks him, incredulous.

Max looks at John. "Who the fuck's Miss Manhattan?"

John looks at Diane. "Who the fuck's Miss Manhattan?"

Diane turns wide, worried eyes on Sophia who shakes her head, discouraged. "I don't know either."

But despite this, Sophia likes large parties. They are more intimate than smaller ones, for here she can wander from the elderly couple dressed as lions, pass two young men costumed as Romeo and Juliet, and Max's youngest daughter disguised as a large dog.

"Sophia," cries a short, animated woman emerging from the dim light wearing a waist coat, velvet britches, white stockings, and slippers. Holding a dueling pistol, tips of her neon-orange hair visible beneath her tricorne hat, Cynthia Sparrow stands very close, kisses Sophia's cheek, and congratulates her "on your mention in the *Times*."

"Only because you exhibited my piece," Sophia replies, then gratefully, "Thank you, Cynthia."

"You're very welcome." She looks with a restless gaze around the crowded room. "We all did well from it," then snaps a glance at her. "Are you at work on something else?"

"Yes."

"In wood again?"

"Yes."

"Good," and Cynthia nods affirmatively. "People like wood."

"That would please my mother."

"What's this new piece?"

"A woman. Well, some of a woman."

"A nude?"

"Yes."

"Good," and Cynthia again looks around the dim, crowded room, "people like nudes. When you're finished let me know."

"Thank you."

"I'll do what I can," then she turns to Sophia, "but you must learn to sell yourself," and moves closer. "Your*self*."

She straightens, her hand indicates the darkened, crowded room, and says with a kind of glory, "Lots of money out there. Max knew how to find it," then she looks at Sophia and nods decisively. "Learn from him."

They both nod at the party, at each other again, then back at the party before Sophia asks, "And might you know who posed for Daniel Chester French?"

Cynthia's head jerks back slightly, she freezes, then asks, "Posed for *who*?"

"Daniel Chester French. He did—"

"No idea," she says with a dismissive frown, and after rising on her toes and a quick kiss though this time on Sophia's lips, Cynthia strides among the frivolity and possibilities.

"You should eat something," Angi tells Sophia while refilling her glass with the good stuff. "Terry coming?"

"He and Pete are heading to Maine."

"So you're mine tonight?"

Sophia lifts a provocative eyebrow, then Angi leans her cheek toward Sophia who gives it a quick peck before weaving again through the dense, costumed gathering. Some guests are familiar to her even in costumes though many are not, and at one point an elderly man dressed as a priest—*Father Duffy?*—softly touches her elbow and with whiskey breath whispers loudly above the chatter, "Have you seen whaz on the walls?" and throws a fearful glance around the loft. "They're gen-wine Max Waters paintings. All of 'em. I shecked the zigture," then, slowly shaking his head in disbelief, whispers loudly, "They mus' be worth a small fortune," and his eyes widen. "No guards, no alarms. You kin jus' walk off with one."

His incredulous gaze remains on one painting and then another before leaning unsteadily closer to Sophia. "Did I say they're jus' hangin' on the walls?"

Sophia assures him he did.

Finally it is time for the costumes to be displayed; the winner takes home an original Max Waters etching of the party with a renowned poet composing extempore an 'occasional poem' across it. Sitting at a card table, the two judges, one with a Hebrew prayer shawl, the other in a wig of long, white curls, and both men wear enormous, yellow eyeglasses meant for clowns. Across from them on a raised platform, a muscular young man in a Speedo swimsuit holds a large beach ball on his shoulders.

"Atlas," someone calls just as David's polaroid flashes.

When the man in the dhoti and holding a staff mounts the platform someone cries, "Gumby" instead of "Gandhi," and "Lincoln in blackface" to the African American poet dressed as Lincoln in tails and a top hat who grudgingly leaves the platform while muttering to the judges, "No statues of any brothers in New York."

A slender woman in a tuxedo and a fedora singing "Give My Regards to Broadway" becomes increasingly irritated after several people yell, "James Cagney," then Cynthia Sparrow takes the spotlight, points her dueling pistol at the ceiling and fires a genuine blank round to the shrieks and startled profanities from guests. A woman in a gown like a Greek goddess lifts a gold crown above her head before the baffled guests who cheer and whistle once Diane drops her robe and remains motionless holding a basket on her thighs as David snaps several polaroids, her naked body briefly illuminated. And no one knows that Audrey Munson had posed for several statues enacted this festive night nor ever heard her name before, not even a costumed *Miss Manhattan*.

∽

WAKING FROM RESTLESS sleep in her cold bed one January morning and certain there is no hot water, Sophia wraps herself in her bed quilt, slips into soft moccasins and, while sipping coffee—the fluorescents bright and buzzing—circles the partially hollowed-out stump where the torso from behind of a naked woman is consumed by the tree. Sophia glares with a critical eye at the swoop down the figure's sides and the upcurved breast, then admits what she knew last night, that *Daphne* is complete and tries feeling happier. She passes her hand along the figure made smooth after hours of sanding with paper coarse and thick down to the finest like a silk stocking which gave the wood almost a soft shine as if lotioned with the moisturizer she uses on her hands and arms. She took a deep, resigned breath knowing her discontent this morning isn't from unsettling dreams or no heat but from the emptiness whenever a piece is done, then she slouches in the shabby lounge chair to stare at her creation an instant before Noel leaps into her lap.

David arrives late that morning.

"This is really cool," he says while snapping several angles of it. "I'll give these to Max," he tells her, "who'll give them to Cynthia Sparrow" who will like what she sees enough to promise displaying it in her spring exhibit which to Sophia seems very far from this cold January day.

Her mornings now feel empty without working on the log, and though wanting to begin a new piece—perhaps a painting of this woman she's pursuing—Sophia returns to the library, so splendid and white, on Fifth Avenue. Up the few stairs to the terrace, through regal Astor Hall, up the grand staircase to the McGraw Rotunda and back to the young, scruffy librarian at the long counter who smiles as she nears.

"Remember me?" she asks, then the librarian holds out a hand while muttering "Remember me remember me," then lifts his head dramatically. " 'The glowworm shows the morning to be near. Adieu, adieu, remember me!' " He then adds casually, "Statues of New York City. Find what you wanted?"

"No. I'm trying to find who *posed* for the statues. Who posed for Daniel Chester French."

After a moment, the librarian says, "Lincoln did, well, sort of."

Sophia considers this. "Not this one."

"Speak with Vinny," and he nods assuredly. "Vinny can help. I'd take you there, but I must" and his voice deepens "*man this desk*," then calls to the desks and low bookcases behind him. "Smith, you got a second? Could you take this young woman over to Vinny?"

Wearing John Lennon-style eyeglasses, with some gray hair left, his work shirt partially untucked, in saggy jeans and a gentle, sleepy smile, Smith rises from behind a bookcase.

He leads Sophia through the Great Reading Room, passing wooden bookshelves and long, glossy tables where a hundred people read beneath banker's lamps with brass stands and green glass shades. There's a curious scent in the huge room, she thinks, *a little like peanut butter*. Smith slows accommodatingly as Sophia's gaze lingers on the long ceiling high above where cherubs float amid sunlit clouds.

"So Heaven is a library," she whispers to Smith who knows just what she means.

A door at one end of the long room leads to an equally beautiful though far smaller Art Division Room where Vinny sits at a table, her head partly shaved, piercings in her ears and one nostril, dressed all in black and turning the pages of a file containing large photographs.

"Vinny," Smith says quietly, "got a customer for you."

She raises her eyes to Sophia and smiles. "Hello."

Smith turns away as Sophia whispers, "Thank you." Vinny soon finds a reference book on Daniel Chester French which must remain in the library, so for a pleasant hour Sophia sits at a long, varnished wood table in a chilly room with two floors of books and a winding staircase in the corner. She turns pages of photographs—the great, seated Lincoln, Columbia University's Alma Mater, her old friends *Miss Manhattan* and *Miss Brooklyn* when still at the Brooklyn entrance of the Manhattan Bridge. There are several of *Memory*, and, to Sophia's surprised delight, a golden woman on Wisconsin's State Capital Building. *Perhaps this woman posed for it,* Sophia wonders, *that I might have been seeing her all my life.* There are photographs of statues of women representing all four continents enthroned before the Custom House on Lower Broadway. There is a photograph of *Mourning Victory* near his *Memory* at the Met, and to her mild shock a bronze Native American woman holding a cornstalk that she admired in Chicago's East Garfield Park though never knowing the sculptor's name.

But there is no mention of who posed for any of the figures except Lincoln himself, a life mask done by Leonard Wells Volk shortly before the first inauguration.

"Volk is named," Sophia mutters irritably, "but not her."

She returns the book to a hopeful Vinny. "Find what you're after?" though Vinny then sees the answer in Sophia's expression.

"Hmm," Vinny says with concern, then more brightly, "so keep searching and maybe I'll see you again."

From the book of outdoor New York sculptures Sophia had noticed female figures on the *Maine Monument* in the southwest corner of Central Park. She'd come to love the park that is a kind of sanctuary in the city as had Lake Michigan for her in Chicago; the Ramble and North Woods even remind her a little of Eagle River only with beer cans and crushed cigarette packs, tissues and condoms, and it was the park that had given her a portion of the tree that would consume her Daphne.

Gently sloping walkways and two grand, scrolled staircases lead to Bethesda Terrace where people stroll around a basin above which an angel hovers, her outstretched hand blessing the pool of water at her feet. Sophia knows the angel descended decades before the woman of her search ever posed for a New York statue, but she quietly asks the handsome face anyway, "Who really are *you*, and are figures of you also all over town and no one knows?"

Had Lily sitting nearby not been softly strumming her mint-green-colored ukelele and singing a simple song—*"On a summer's evening"*—but heard Sophia's question, she could have told her the story about the angel's model Charlotte Cushman, "the greatest actress of her day," then open wide her lively, brown eyes "and lover of the angel's sculptor, Emma Stebbins." Exaggerating her shock, she'd add, "Scandalous more than a century ago!"

But Lily never heard Sophia's question to the angel—*"While Tony played the organ"*— as Sophia drops a dollar in Lily's open uke case and the two women exchange smiles before Sophia moves on.

The *Maine Monument* is a tall, imposing tower of stone blocks with bigger-than-life figures as if from ancient Greece lounging along the sides of a stone boat's bow. To Sophia, it all seems clumsy and overbearing for an entrance to such a pleasant park. At the tower's base, a gowned woman stands with her arms extended to the city, palms down as if in blessing. Sophia climbs the bow of the boat to see more closely the figure's face, and she thinks this too might be the woman of her searching.

Behind the stone tower, facing the park, another woman, gowned and hooded, her bare arms extended, palms upward, and—Sophia's sure of it—the same woman in the boat. And if able to rise forty feet she'd see the same face again atop the tower, gold and gowned, one hand upraised holding a victory wreath, the other reigning three wild horses. Carved into the monument's stone base, ATTILIO PICCIRILLI SCULPTOR. Sophia rolls the name in her mind before remembering with a jolt that it is carved into the firemen's monument on Riverside Drive.

To the gentle figure with arms reaching for the park—palms upward as if in celebration— Sophia whispers, "I *know* you."

∽

ON A COLD, drizzly afternoon in early spring, Terry and Sophia deliver from her storefront to the Sparrow Gallery on Prince Street a blanket-wrapped *Daphne* for the coming exhibition. Cynthia Sparrow diligently oversees the placement and setting of each work for aesthetic value and, with the pieces now in her gallery, for which she is responsible.

"Sophia," she calls while approaching with busy agitation, "who is this handsome man?"

Sophia introduces them as Cynthia rises on tiptoes and Terry bends to a kiss on his cheek.

"So you *do* know," Cynthia declares, "you are the luckiest man in New York" though before he replies she says with annoyance, "Now unwrap this piece I haven't yet seen," then adds tenderly, "and be gentle. Wood is delicate. It was once alive."

When the severed tree trunk absorbing the woman is unwrapped, Cynthia glares at it intensely.

"Very nice," she says, nodding several times before turning her eyes to Sophia, "very nice."

Cynthia again rises on her toes to kiss first Sophia and then Terry goodbye, then they leave the gallery and walk a wet Wooster Street to Terry's truck. There, she presses against him, then bends back her head as he dips for a kiss.

"See you tonight?" she says.

"I'll come to you."

"My bed's too small."

"All the better," Terry says, "and it's really Noel I want to see. Climb in I'll give you a ride back to work."

"I want to walk."

"It's *rain*ing."

"I *like* the rain," and she squints at the gray sky, "and it's only a drizzle."

They kiss again as he presses her against him.

After he climbs into the truck's cab, she says, "Thank you," then adds dramatically, "How can I *ever* repay you?"

Terry shoves the stick shift in gear, and after a thoughtful moment replies, "Sleep with me" before she says with feigned unhappiness, "Oh, alright," as the truck rubbles along the damp, cobblestone street.

In a newsboy cap and her old leather jacket, Sophia tucks herself a little deeper into her scarf and hurries along Soho's nearly deserted sidewalks, passing galleries and designer boutiques and a grim, graffitied loading dock. She crosses West Houston Street and into Washington Square, its trees bare and black, and wonders if any students passing through are hurrying to art class to sketch a posing, struggling dreamer. With a soft smile for her former self, she stretches out an arm, then moves her hand to her heart in gratitude to the city giving her so much.

Along a narrow block to the east is a platform with a table on it where three people sit, a few others standing before it silent and wet. A small bell is being tapped repeatedly, a brief pause between each tap. During the ceremonial tappings, people glance upward to the top floors of the old ten-story building behind the table, and after many taps of the bell, "May the souls of all one-hundred-and-forty-six of these victims," utters somberly the man who had tapped the bell, "rest eternally in peace." He gestures to the building behind him. "And because of what happened here eighty years ago today, this building is now a national historic landmark. May such a tragedy never again happen in New York."

The small gathering slowly disperses though Sophia remains, glancing at the top floors as the tappings of the bell fade in the chilly afternoon.

She wonders what happened here eighty years ago where so many died, and why people were lifting their eyes to the top floors of that somber building. She knows there's a dark story here and wants to learn it but then shakes her head with irritation; she hasn't found even the *name* of this woman for whom she's searching, this Miss Manhattan. She hurries to the Old Master's studio, but the solemn ceremony won't leave her, then she realizes that the woman she seeks was posing eighty years ago—"*Some of those girls were pretty too.*" An artist's model, the woman of her search had surely walked these same sidewalks when this neighborhood was New York's Left Bank, the woman's footsteps mixed in the rain with the inaudible taps of the bell.

Impatient to find who this woman is and begin some new piece about her, Sophia returns to the library where Vinny finds a journal article on the Piccirilli Brothers. In the cool, quiet Art Division Room Sophia reads about Attilio and Furio's workshop in the Bronx, that they had carved the formidable, contented lions on the library's terrace and had worked often with Daniel Chester French. The connection fortifies Sophia's belief that the same woman posed for all the brothers' statues. She even reads Attilio's obituary from a Poughkeepsie newspaper, but missing is the name of the model who posed for much of Piccirilli's work.

"Still nothing?" Vinny whispers. "Hmm." Her eyebrows press together, but after a moment's worry she brightens. "So the search continues!"

The next morning Sophia calls the Museum of the City of New York and leaves a voice message. Days pass and she calls again, leaves the same message, and receives a reply the next day on her answering machine. The museum staff doesn't know the model's name but suggests she try the New York Historical Society. She does; after several days there's a reply on her machine to "Try Landmarks Preservation."

Sophia didn't know Landmarks Preservation was established so another loss like Pennsylvania Station never again happens in New York City, nor did she even know that there had ever been such a magnificent train station decades earlier. Several more days pass before Sophia gets a message stating that Landmarks doesn't know the name of the model nor has any knowledge that this same woman for whom Sophia searches modeled for the graceful, provocative figures once paralleling the wreathed-encircled clocks atop demolished Pennsylvania Station.

Sophia asks the Old Master if he knows anyone at the Metropolitan Museum of Art who might find the name of the model for French's *Memory* and his *Mourning Victory* in the museum's American Wing. Max knows a curator there and asks, but a week later he tells Sophia, "The curator doesn't know but most likely someone will at the Museum of the City of New York."

SPRING ARRIVES, THE real spring of flowers opening and the scent of green on warm breezes as life in the city truly begins again. Max invited Sophia to the opening of his exhibition at the Marlborough Gallery on West 57th Street. On its large patio, lavish trays of cut vegetables with various dips crowd beside crackers, sliced French bread, four different wines, and a colorful, outrageous cartoon-version three-dimensional *Brooklyn Bridge* by Red Grooms so large Sophia can walk across it. She wears her Western boots that night and a form-fitting, black dress. John and Diane attend, and even David and Kylie were freed "only briefly," moaned David in a white tuxedo, "from the studio dungeon." Sophia recognizes people she'd met through Max, and some recognize her, and to her amazement the man at the costume party who had been so concerned about the paintings on the walls is still dressed as a priest, which he must be after all.

The opening at the Sparrow Gallery soon follows. Terry and Pete were delivering a handmade wooden arc to a synagogue in a Chicago suburb, Angi had rehearsal, and since Max attended her first gallery showing he thought that was enough. But Sophia has a fine time anyway despite being too nervous to eat and limiting herself to a single glass of wine after believing everything she said to the other guests seemed ridiculous. She hadn't seen her *Daphne* since Terry and she had delivered it to the gallery weeks ago and is now a little surprised how large and formidable it is, that and how beautiful. Standing a good distance away, she watches as visitors pause before it, nodding a while then moving on while others linger and look at the piece from various angles. Proud, discreet, she creeps closer and passes her hand lightly across the figure's smooth, bare shoulder.

A few weeks later Max invites her to stay at a guest house on his property in Southampton so that she might attend the Parrish Gallery opening. There is a swimming pool in the backyard, but with the ocean three blocks away she walks the shoreline's pale sand in a black one-piece. After slowly wading up to her knees in water less chilly than Cranberry Lake she dives into an incoming wave, tasting salt water for the first time. While drifting with the swells she feels Earth's breath with each incoming and receding wave.

Back in New York Sophia broods for days on what she can do next to find this woman all over town. Nearly a year has passed since that summer night seeing *Memory* at the Met, and though she remains resolute her sorrow deepens for this woman who had given so much to the city yet remains so unknown; since returning from Southampton, Sophia has had repeated, unsettling imagines of a woman in the ocean drifting from sight.

She calls the Central Park Conservancy; after all, there are two statues of this model on the *Maine Monument*—and a third had she risen up the tower to the golden figure above. The Conservancy transfers her to the park's historian, and Sophia is gratefully amazed to be talking to a person. But unfortunately, Sarah also doesn't know the name of the model though feels certain "the Museum of the City of New York will."

Sophia returns to the library for a book on the statues of Central Park; though unlikely, perhaps the model's name is mentioned.

The scruffy librarian peruses the database. "Catnip," he says to it, "bring me good fortune!" And for the next hour Sophia sits in a metal chair on the library terrace across from the pale, sensuous nude in the alcove while reading the slender *The Central Park Book* but again finds nothing about this elusive woman.

Leaving for the day and heading to a bar nearby, gentle-faced Smith notices Sophia, hesitates, then approaches.

"How's your search going?"

Looking up, Sophia asks, "Did you know that there is not a single statue in Central Park of a real woman? There's an angel, one of Alice in wonderland, actually *two* of her, and three dancing maidens, maybe the three graces, but not a real woman."

She closes the book, disheartened. "Not very well. And I don't know where to look next."

"For what?"

"For the name of the model who posed for Daniel Chester French's Miss Manhattan and Miss Brooklyn."

Smith nods slowly.

"And his Memory at the Met," Sophia declares. After a breath, she adds with less certainty, "And for a few others around town."

Smith looks at her a moment. "Are you a reporter or grad student?"

"No," she cries. "I just want to know who this woman *is*."

She shakes her head, then with rising irritation, "We know the sculptors, but who is *she*?"

Smith nods several more times, then says slowly, "June 8th, 1913, The New York Sun." His head tilts back toward the library. "It's on microfilm," then again clearly and slow, "The New York Sun," and repeats the date. Before leaving, he turns to the statue of *Beauty* in the alcove behind him, then to Sophia, "And doesn't she look familiar?"

Sophia's eyes follow him a moment, then she looks at the white, naked woman leaning against a horse, the figure's glance and right arm uplifted. She hurries back in the library, and after cranking through a plastic spool of black microfilm smelling like vinegar, she finds this—

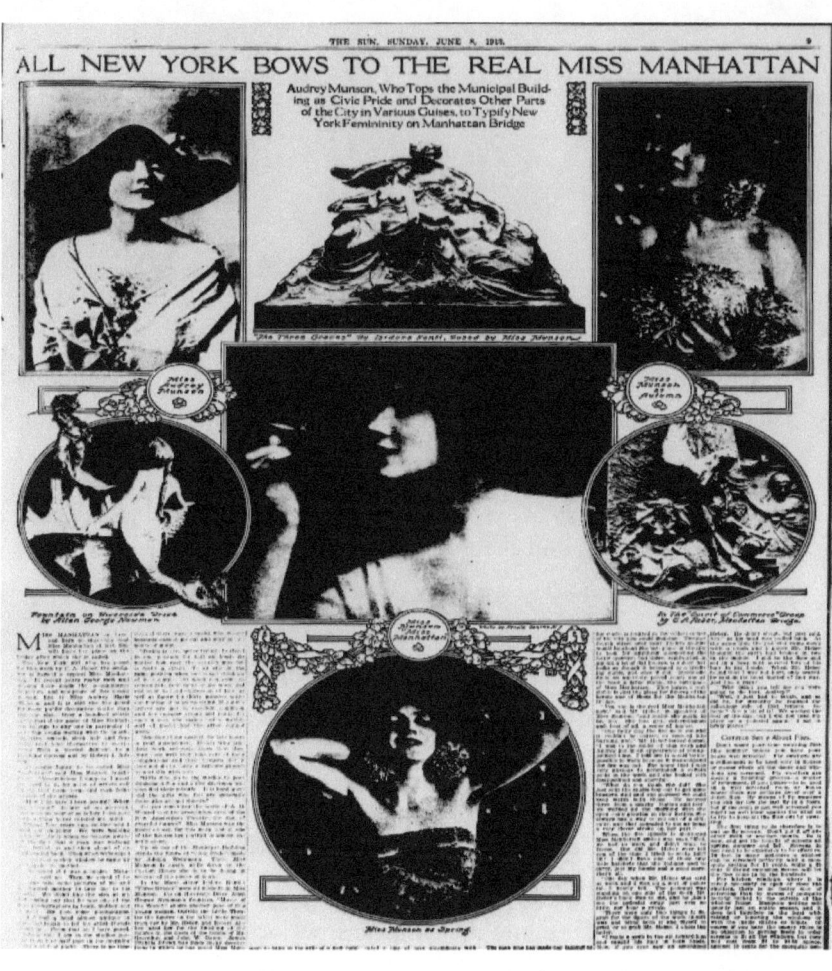

# Chapter Five

Slipping slowly through cold, gray-white mist, its foghorn bellowing a deep, long note spreading solitary and foreboding through New York's Upper Bay, SS *Chicago* very slowly sailed into port, her hull a black, floating mountain. Smells of smoke and oil as seagulls screeched, and then quick *toot-toot* from ferryboats invisible where the ocean muddled with the river slightly darker than the gray-white mist.

Once past the Battery, another *toot* and another, then long moans of a steamboat's horn and a heavy-tongued bell to portside. The stink of rank vegetables, wet ash, rotted flesh, sweat, and rarely—what lifted each sailor's head who caught a whiff—a soft wind carried downriver the scent from three hundred miles of pure forest to the north.

Soon the mighty tugboats were at work, nudging the tremendous black hull bow and stern into the long, narrow dock among long, narrow docks of splintered planks in putrid water where bottles and rags bobbed in greasy bubbles with fish heads large as cats. A colossal rattling of heavy chain, then thigh-thick ropes fore and aft loop over bollards that dock the great ship. Leaner rope and tackle from iron cranes below deck soon lifted from the hold nets haphazardly filled with wood crates lowered to the dock and sturdy longshoremen with strong, damaged shoulders dragging, lugging, and stacking crate upon crate in a vast warehouse, each crate with a stenciled name—

**Van Gogh Cezanne Brancusi Picasso**

Crates stack on crates while from the ship's deep hold more nets rose, pass slowly, creaking overhead before descending to leather-gloved hands of those men pushing, guiding, and lifting each stenciled crate—

**Monet Lautrec Duchamps Matisse**

Beyond the warehouse, a mountain-range of dark, straight lines and angles amid infernal, constant smoke ever-rising, a veil over the sun.

EARLY ONE MILD February afternoon Rozie puffed casually on a pre-rolled cigarette outside the locked gate on the uptown side of tidy Gramercy Park. Slender, small-breasted, slim-hipped, hers would be the perfect figure for the feminine ideal soon to come. In a new bob–her dark, wavy hair cut to jaw level—dressed smartly in a tapered black coat well below her knees, seemingly aloof, she gazed at the black cars and carriages arriving three blocks up Lexington Avenue to the armory and felt the excitement of this event even from Gramercy Park.

Seeing Audrey's graceful stride a half-block west, Rozie had another quick puff before dropping the cigarette into the gutter, and from a small packet in a small pocket of her coat put a Sen-Sen mint on the tip of her tongue. She quickly dabbed eau de cologne on her crimson-colored cashmere scarf, then pushed her hand back into her thin leather glove as both young women reached for the other's hand and eager, quick kisses.

"I love your bob!" Audrey cried in happy surprise, then she threw a glance to the leafless trees above them. "What a fine day for this," Audrey said, her eyes lively and wide and turning toward the commotion up Lexington Avenue. She took Rozie's arm in hers and whispered after one step, "And put some in your hair." Rozie turned with an embarrassed, grateful smile as they crossed East 23rd Street arms entwined.

They were young, lovely, stylish, confident, each wearing a felt hat,

Rozie's crimson cloche tilted lower to one side, Audrey's with a small brim the color as her blue-gray eyes. They appeared nearly the same height, though Audrey was two inches taller, her shoes having only a slight heel while Rozie's boots had a high arch. They were accustomed to attention along the streets of New York, and strolling together so contentedly their allure shone even brighter. Audrey looked straight ahead, a faint smile as if holding a pose, her long, black hair along her shoulders, but Rozie's dark eyes sought those of the admirers, the envious, the gawkers, a camera, a small smile curled in one corner of her lips. As they neared the steps of the colossal fortress-like 69th Regiment Armory beneath a banner—

### INTERNATIONAL EXHIBITION
### OF
### MODERN ART

— Audrey looked across Lexington to the dozen women behind a barricade and heard their determined calls of "Modern art for modern women!"

"Aren't they wonderful?" she cried with exuberance.

Rozie glanced disinterested at the small demonstration.

"So why not join them?"

"I did," Audrey declared, then strode up the few wide steps through the great entrance. "I give a day's pay each month to the Cause."

"Does your mother know?"

"Yes," then added above a stage whisper, "just not how much."

The drill-space of the vast 69th Regiment Armory was large as a football field enclosed by formidable walls with a towering, vaulted, iron-beamed ceiling where enormous chandeliers hung by chains, each link thick as a finger. The chandeliers lit sculptures set on pedestals and platforms and garland-trimmed partitions where paintings were displayed; between them a hundred spectators strolled. The 69th Regimental Band continuously played light waltzes, a soft rendition of the popular "Alexander's Ragtime Band," and always after several melodies the trumpet-heralding "Promenade" from Mussorgsky's *Pictures at an Exhibition*. From those viewing the artwork came an agitated "Outrageous" and a haunting "Beautiful" and from an older woman with amused distain to a canvas "Perhaps it is a map of the Balkan Mountains" just before the hardy, emphatic "Ha!" thrown to the ceiling from the young man beside her.

Audrey was having a wonderful time and feeling not merely a visitor but a participant, an artist among other artists in this startling, controversial exhibition with her own image displayed in the American section. But among the brightly colored canvases, the marble and the bronze, she felt that people looking at her whispered as she passed; one person even pointed a discreet finger her direction. When she heard her name muttered, she laughed to herself, and a blush colored her fair cheeks.

"Do you hear what they *call* you?" Rozie asked excitedly as they wound through the crowded partitions.

"Isn't it silly," she replied, delighted.

"American *Venus*?"

"Only my arms and hands," Audrey insisted. "The rest is pure Venus de Milo."

She stopped before a canvas one yard high, then asked with confusion, "Does she have three—"

"Apparently," Rozie said with casual dismay but added irritably, "and where is her *face*?"

Audrey leaned toward the small bronze plaque beside it. *Standing Female Nude* Picasso.

"You know what the papers say about this show," Rozie confided as they strolled on. "The armory's war on art." The two laughed before Audrey repeated what she'd heard amid the plaster dust in artists' studios. "Well *now* it seems," and she returned a nod from someone unknown to her, "in New York, as in France, that cubism and these other *isms* have become quite the fad."

A young man stepped in her way and snapped a photo with his Leica 35mm, and then a quick one of Rozie as the heralding trumpet announcing the "Promenade" played again.

"And one together?" he begged as Audrey glanced slightly to one side and Rozie looked directly into the lens.

They continued among canvases, a nude woman in blue— "My God," Rozie cried, "is that the way some of them see us?"—one of green and brown splotches, another with wedges and lines and half-circles, then a delicate watercolor of the newly completed Woolworth Building. Rozie tilted her head and looked at a charcoal drawing resembling a twisted birdcage titled *Cityscape* and laughed. "Just like home," she said to it, and after passing a canvas of a standing woman, fleshy, realistic, and nude—"Now *this* I like"—Audrey paused before a painting of a nude woman lying in a meadow. She straightened slightly and threw a glance, eyebrows uplifted, at Rozie before moving on.

"He changed the color of your hair," Rozie protested.

"So you see," Audrey told her friend as they continued their comfortable stroll, "not *all* the artists have lost their minds." She paused at a naked man in bronze, his weight on his bent right leg, his left extended out to the side, an immense bow in his left hand without string and arrow, his eyes focused in the distance. For a moment Audrey imagined the difficulty of the pose and the model's endurance, but she was drawn to the sensual power without the least vulnerability in his nakedness. Her gaze moved along his throat, his muscular torso, and the penis flaccid and thick.

"Miss Munson," Audrey heard beside her, then turned to a tall man with a full mustache and intense, green eyes. She extended her hand.

"Mr. MacMoonies. How nice to see you."

He struggled suppressing a smile as he glanced from Audrey to Rozie.

"Rosaline Spear," Audrey said to him, then to Rozie, "Frederick MacMoonies" and the two shook hands, MacMoonies bowing slightly.

"Mr. MacMoonies," Audrey told Rozie, "sculpted the two figures on the public library's terrace."

He bowed slightly to Audrey with quiet gratitude as Rozie asked with a raised eyebrow, "Do you like what you see here today?"

"Captivating." His gaze remained on her before adding, "Are you a model as well?"

"Yes," and she laughed lightly, "but photography. You sculptors take far too long."

An elderly man unknown to Audrey touched her elbow in passing; she smiled, nodded in return, and felt like a celebrity.

"How do you *do* this?" Rozie whispered after she and Audrey parted from MacMoonies. "How do you pose *naked* before these men?"

With exaggerated triumph, Audrey declared, her chin lifting slightly, "I brazen it out!"

She liked the word and had found times to say it ever since the suffragettes proudly referred to themselves this way after the newspapers called them "brazen streetwalkers."

"In front of old Konti I understand," Rozie said placing a hand on Audrey's arm, "but how do you *brazen it out* before that handsome man?"

Audrey considered this for a moment.

"While holding a pose," she said, "I think of myself only as an object in marble or bronze."

She spoke with assurance, for she had thought carefully about her posing, which even to herself at times seemed bold and nearly shameless. But she believed herself an artist, and what art created spread outward to people, deepening their lives; she felt proud of herself for it, this life of value guiding her and, to her delight, this new recognition.

"I am only one girl," she said, "but as a statue I can represent many," then she stopped, closed her eyes, and said, "I begin as an idea in the mind of the sculptor," then opened her eyes, "and he's trying to make me real."

With her chin slightly uplifted, she took Rozie's arm in hers and continued along their casual way until Audrey paused at a pedestal displaying a woman's marble torso a foot high.

"Like this poor girl," Audrey said, "only with arms and legs."

She spoke confidently, even with faint superiority, not to Rozie but to those in fine bonnets and top hats among which she strolled.

"But if I'm in the altogether, then the moment he puts down his pencil I'm human again, a little embarrassed, and cover up quickly."

Rozie threw another searching glance behind her. "Well he can see *my* body if he likes."

Among the partitions and pedestals—"Ridiculous," someone declared, and "It's pronounced Bran-coosh," said another, and from a young man standing before a large poster in yellow and red for a cabaret, "Isn't he that little cripple who painted prostitutes?"—visitors sat contemplatively on benches or struggled to understand strange shapes or lingered on a dim, realistic painting inside *McSorley's Bar*. Only a few steps away, Audrey saw Isidore Konti gazing at a painting, his troubled eyes brightening at the sight of her.

"Audrey, my dear!" He extended a hand and lightly kissed her cheek, "how wonderful to see you. And Miss Spears," he said happily to Rozie. "Look at you two!"

"And only moments ago," Rozie declared with a small smile, "Audrey was telling me how she can pose—"

"And what," Audrey interrupted with a sharp glance at Rozie, "does my dear mentor think of what he sees here today?"

Gradually Konti's face drained of joy, then he gazed across the exhibition thoughtfully.

"Here is a new way of looking at the world," and he nodded slowly, "a torch passed from one age to the next as art always must to thrive."

Konti looked at Audrey, then with a kind of exhaustion he pointed at the painting before them.

"Does this look familiar?" he asked. "Elegance, mirth, youthful beauty?"

To Audrey the painting resembled a shattered window of many colors carelessly reassembled.

"And now," Konti said heavily, "this too is the Three Graces."

He nodded slowly several times at the canvas, then shook his head before looking at Audrey and Rozie with renewed vitality.

"My dear young ladies," and his hand, palm upward, indicated the partition, then the entire armory, "the new world awaits you."

Konti smiled with effort and bowed slightly before moving on through the crowd. Audrey's eyes remained on him as Rozie said quietly, "Audrey look" and strained to better see the small group gathered around a spectator observing a painting. He was large chested, in a dark three-piece suit, a full mustache, with pince-nez eyeglasses and an aura of success. "That's Theodore Roosevelt."

Audrey had far more concern for Konti but threw a quick glance in the direction of this puffed-up man she'd never liked for famously slaughtering animals on safari.

"Where's the nude?" a top-hatted elderly man asked the gathering. "Does anyone see a nude?"

"I can't even see a *stair*case," declared a woman in a fur.

"It resembles," Roosevelt said with conviction as those around him waited, "the Navajo rug on my bathroom floor."

He laughed tremendously, then everyone laughed tremendously, and this spread to those nearby except for a young Marcel Duchamp slouched at the edge as Audrey kept searching for Konti lost amid the partitions, the pedestals, and the future he feared that February afternoon in 1913.

∽

MONUMENTAL WORKS WERE underway for the entrances to the newly completed Manhattan Bridge, its lofty towers not granite blocks that recall an enduring past but light, graceful steel beams of the future. Having completed the elegant, white-marble library on Fifth Avenue, John Carrère and Thomas Hastings envisioned for the entrance to the bridge on the Manhattan side a triumphant arch reminiscent of Paris, columns extending from both sides of the roadways and for which tenements vanished, thousands of New Yorkers lugging their burdens deeper into the dense city.

For the Brooklyn entrance to the bridge, Daniel Chester French will set on pylons paralleling each side of the roadway two granite women robed and enthroned, each twelve-feet high, Miss Manhattan and Miss Brooklyn.

"Although sitting regally with garlands on her head," French told Audrey in his studio bright with morning sunlight, "Miss Brooklyn is modest, reflective. We begin with her."

For hours French sketched Audrey seated on a wooden armchair, one arm placed this way, then another way, the heavy robe gradually more oppressive that warm morning. He circled her slowly, sketching all the time. "Try this," French said, and she did, and "Head lower" as sketches on thick paper fell to the floor.

In one accustomed pause from their work, Audrey and French sat in mismatched stuffed chairs before a low table with tea, light cakes, and slices of fruit. Audrey dropped the robe from her shoulders, closed her eyes and slowly stretched her neck to one side, then the other side, then arched her back and stayed that way a while. While watching her, French decided that when these large figures were complete, he would do a bust of Audrey, her neck and shoulders bare.

"I believe it's providential," French said, his eyes brightening, "that the young woman inspiring these works representing New York City was born elsewhere. After all," and he smiled with delight, "even The Statue of Liberty is from elsewhere."

He paused a moment, his eyes on Audrey. "Rochester, isn't it?"

"I remember only a dirty little town," she laughed sadly.

"I too am from a dirty little town," he assured her, "in New Hampshire. And now here we are," and his eyes widened, "in the most exciting city in the world, together creating Miss Brooklyn and Miss Manhattan."

Audrey shook her head quietly astonished. "I'm having dreams come true that I never dreamed."

After a moment he said calmly, "You are quite extraordinary. There is no monotony in your expression. Always changing. And it is of great satisfaction to find this in one with such grace and finesse of line combined."

He leaned closer. "I am lucky to have found you."

His words sent a rush of pride upward from her heart, a confirmation of her worth from a great artist. And while touched by French's compliment Audrey also felt humbled, grateful not only to French but to the spirit guiding her remarkable path; she thrilled at how blessed she was for these gifts from French, this city, and her guiding spirit.

After a few moments, French asked, "Can you go on a little longer?"

"Whatever you need me to do," she replied, and though she posed for another two hours, French would spend the next three days glaring repeatedly at these sketches for the right pose of the figure.

"Miss Manhattan is proud," he declared one morning as Audrey in the heavy gown once again arranged herself in the wooden chair as he sketched rapidly and she slowly varied her poses, "queen of the kingdom."

Imagining herself truly New York's adored figure, Audrey raised her chin as if a queen endowed to rule; she set her face with an attitude of superiority, even looking slightly down at the world, then bent her left arm and placed a fist on her thigh, exalted, defiant.

"Yes," French cried quietly to himself, "hubris!"

Audrey hadn't been invited to the dedication of the Ida and Isidor Straus memorial at 106th Street, not to the solemn ceremony on Riverside Drive honoring New York's firemen nor when the scaffolding was removed from Weinman's *Civic Fame* atop the Municipal Building. But Daniel Chester French insisted she be invited to the dedications of *Miss Brooklyn* and *Miss Manhattan* held at the Brooklyn entrance to the Manhattan Bridge. In a form-fitting, lace dress of pale blue, a lavender shawl and a matching wide brimmed hat, Audrey hoped after that day for the public to finally acknowledge how she too was an artist in the same way a contralto is for the composer. *Without me*—and her shaded, exhilarated eyes scanned the gathering—*the sculptures*, as Konti had once said to her, *would be merely a face without a heart.*

For three hours on a clear day in early June, the roadway on the Brooklyn side of the new bridge to Manhattan closed to accommodate dignitaries, newspaper reporters and photographers, and guests seated at the entrance to the bridge. Its designer, Leon Moussaieff, could not attend, instead surveying a project in the West though not his bridge over the Tacoma Narrows that would in time sway with *torsional flutter* before collapsing in the cold water of Puget Sound.

The gathering on the Manhattan Bridge was paralleled by two regal women carved in granite, twelve-feet high and seated enthroned on elaborate pedestals. *Miss Manhattan* was to the right of the roadway, *Miss Brooklyn* to the left. Brooklyn Borough President Alfred Steers welcomed this stone figure; she is grand, graceful, modest, her chin lowered, a child reading nestled beside her. Manhattan Borough President George McAneny welcomed *Miss Manhattan,* a peacock beside that figure, chin uplifted as she proudly scans her domain. Both figures were greeted with light, sustained applause.

In tails and top hat, New York City Mayor William Gaynor spoke for nearly an hour even with the bullet still lodged in his throat from an assassination attempt three years before. From her folding chair Audrey looked across the city to her left, to the gleaming figure of herself at the pinnacle of the Municipal Building visible from the entryway of the new bridge. With a buoyant breath she felt as if she truly *were* the great city's queen of a sort, its Miss Manhattan and Miss Brooklyn, then with her fingertip she began tracing an imaginary path of her own wondrous journey. Sands Street to one side and Jay Street to the other leading to the bridge were her Rochester and Providence. The roadway curved upward, gradually rising straight and true like her success as the artists' model, then her fingertip touched the first of the distant towers of blue steel high above the river. *This is where I am*, she thought, and she could see beyond the tower to the roadway steadily rising and knew a rising path awaited her.

After Daniel Chester French thanked the mayor, the borough presidents, the gathered audience, his gifted, tireless assistants "freed from the studio for just one day," his hand gestured to Audrey.

"There is the *real* Miss Manhattan," he declared, and her heart surged as a flush rose to her face. "She is beautiful, has grit and stamina," and Audrey nodded thankfully to the light applause around her, her heart pounding so quickly that she worried her breasts were fluttering, "and like many of us comes from somewhere else. And these statues for which she posed," and he gestured to the figures he had created, "shall forever remain here, giving welcome as Miss Manhattan and Miss Brooklyn to those crossings in the great city of the New World."

After the ceremonies and speeches, no photographs of *Miss Brooklyn* or *Miss Manhattan* appeared in the June 8, 1913, *The New York Sun*—but at the top of a full page with four photographs of Audrey and one of Konti's *Three Graces* from the Hotel Astor three years before was the headline—

**ALL NEW YORK BOWS TO THE REAL MISS MANHATTAN**

She had posed for Manhattan's tallest statue on the largest office building in the world. High on the *Maine Monument,* she reigned wild horses, bestowed peace from the bow of its boat, and behind the tower as the shrouded figure with arms raised in abundance to Central Park. Her figure was the pale, sensuous nude in the public library alcove, she symbolized *Day* and *Night* on the wreathed-encircled clock for all travelers entering imperial Pennsylvania Station, was both pensive and steadfast for firemen on Riverside Drive, lovely and reflective for the Straus couple nearby. And for what Audrey believed kismet, serendipitous, an affirmation of her destiny, the *Sun* article appeared on her twenty-second birthday.

But from her folding chair on that bright day of the ceremony, Audrey could not see that the steady rise of the roadway had a summit, that the deck then descended. Nor could she imagine that—like her fingertip journey—she had reached her own summit, that her finest days were already behind her in the vast, ever-changing city that she loved.

# Chapter Six

Sitting in a metal chair on the library terrace one late-spring morning across from the pale, sensuous nude in the alcove, Sophia realizes that something taught to her at the Art Institute in Chicago has been reversed. She'd learned that seeing a living person is seeing only a single human being, but in marble or bronze the person represents a portion of humanity. Now, for Sophia, the opposite is also true. Each statue is no longer *Memory* or *Miss Manhattan* but rather this singular woman, Audrey Munson—she now at last knows her name—who has so enriched New York. She looks at the searching, upturned face and wonders what Audrey was thinking, if the studio was chilly in February or stifling in August, where did she live, had she a lover. When the library's great bronze doors open Sophia is the first one standing before the surprised, shaggy librarian.

"What, returned so soon," he cries, then gestures with an open palm to the arch window behind her, "when yet the clock hath not strucken twelve upon the hill?"

Sophia places her fist emphatically on her hip. "Some half-dozen words with your kinsman Smith."

Sleepy, disheveled, and smiling, Smith rises from his desk. "I *thought* I'd see you soon."

"Now what?" she wonders.

He mulls this over a moment. "I have lunch at one, Mulligan's on Madison near 39th. Meet me there and I'll explain."

Sophia visits the library gift shop looking at bookends of the library lions, notebooks with fine leather covers, the glass display case of thick fountain pens, ivory broaches and sparkling pins of dragonflies. She delicately lifts the tip of a scarf hanging on a rack that unfolds to reveal the exterior of the library with images of the lions and the two sculptures *Truth* and *Beauty* along the terrace. She buys it, wraps it around her shoulders, and soon sips a vodka martini at the bar in Mulligan's beside Smith munching a burger and fries with a shot of Jack Daniels on the rocks.

"We just thought it was a rest home," he says. "Granma was in a *rest* home. Not until later did I realize it was the Saint Lawrence Institute for the Insane even though the *fucking name* is right above the entrance. Pardon my Daniel Chester."

Smith hesitates, then points to his plate. "And help yourself to the fries" as Sophia quickly snatches one.

"We visited Granma near Christmas and on Mother's Day and each summer for her birthday. We lived only a couple hours away. It was *fine* at Saint Lawrence. No crazy people yelling, no straightjackets, nothing like in the movies. It was a *rest* home. I never really understood why Granma was even there. Something about her *burdened spirit* from what happened to Granpa during the war. But she was sweet and funny and always happy to see us."

Smith pushes the plate away just as Sophia takes another fry, then asks her, "One more?" indicating her drink. She declines as he says to the bartender, "Another Jack."

"And there was an old woman everyone referred to as the celebrity," Smith continued. " 'She's our celebrity,' Granma told us. She was older than Granma and kept to herself. Always nicely dressed, often brushing her long, gray hair. She read a lot. I liked that. I didn't know anything about her, but the nurses were very fond of Miss Audrey. That's what everyone called her. Even Granma called her that."

When the whiskey arrives Sophia snatches another fry just before the bartender takes the plate.

"I'm a research librarian," Smith resumes after a sip, "so it didn't take long to find out who she was. And in all the times we visited Granma she never had a visitor. Ever."

He takes another, slower sip. "That was some thirty years ago."

Sophia broods on this while sipping her martini, then asks, "What happened to your grandfather?"

Smith shakes his head, irritated and amused.

"Died in a plane crash," Smith says, "a *training* accident," then more animated. "The guy fought through Africa, Sicily, the Battle of the Bulge, the war in Europe's over and he dies in a fucking *training* accident while waiting for his big boat home."

Smith's anger simmers after another sip.

"If *I* were young and in love," Sophia says quietly, "that would burden my spirit too."

∽

WITH TERRY ACROSS from her at the small table beneath her platform bed, Sophia dials information for Ogdensburg, New York, then asks for the number of The Saint Lawrence Hospital for the Insane though there is no listing.

"I have The Saint Lawrence Psychiatric Center," the operator says hopefully.

"That will be fine, thank you," and Sophia smiles at Terry, eyebrows lifting for an instant. Once connected to the receptionist Sophia says, "Good afternoon. My name is Sophia Bauer and I'm calling to find out about someone who was once a patient there."

"The patient's name?"

"Audrey Munson."

Silence.

"Hello?" Sophia says.

"The hospital does not give out any patient information."

"I only want to—" and the receptionist repeats the policy about patient information.

"Please," Sophia says with quiet urgency, "this woman is very important to me," adding quickly, "very dear," and she takes a breath. "Perhaps there is a place I could lay some flowers," then laughs unhappily, "if I only knew where."

Another silence, but when the receptionist speaks again her voice has softened.

"Let me put you on hold," and she does so, then calls for a nurse's attendant. After hearing the message the nurse walks swiftly and quietly a flight of wide, carpeted stairs to the sunlit ward. There is a gathering of several people for an old woman in bed with a small package in her lap. "Oh thank you," says the old woman, and "How pretty" and "Open it Granma" which she does slowly with arthritic hands unsteady and ringless and thin.

"Excuse me, Mrs. Elliot," whispers the nurse, "there's a matter for your attention."

Beneath the pink ribbon and white wrapping paper, a box of finely polished wood that when opened plays the first, sweet metallic notes of "The Sidewalks of New York." The soft sound drifts above the clean linoleum floor, passed the beds with their dozing patients, the melody slowing, expending towards the distant window where a squirrel has leaped to the ledge.

Large, elderly, well-groomed, Mrs. Elliot excuses herself from the small gathering and hurries to the phone with the nurse who, hushed and troubled, says, "Someone asking about Miss Audrey" and Mrs. Elliot bristles.

"Hello," she snaps into the receiver.

"Yes, hello." Sophia gives her name again. "I'm trying to find—"

"And why do you believe this person is here?"

Sophia momentarily freezes. "Excuse me?"

"Why do you believe this person is here? Are you a relative?"

After a fumbling instant, Sophia says, "An aunt."

Mrs. Elliot laughs. "Most unlikely," then declares, "We do not divulge any information about patients."

"All I'm—" and Mrs. Elliot repeats herself more emphatically before hanging up.

At the table beneath her platform bed, with Sophia's focus remaining on the phone, Terry asks, "So, do you know where she is?"

Quietly amazed, Sophia lifts her eyes to him. "I think she's *there*."

"They told you that?"

"They told me nothing."

"Then why—"

"Because the woman asked what makes you think she is a patient here. Not *was* a patient here but *is* a patient here."

Sophia looks at the phone again, her face distraught, nods several times and declares, "I'm going there."

"Ogdensburg? You know where that is? That's almost Canada."

"There must be a train or bus," and she smiles, "or a horse."

"And *this* on the tense of a verb?"

He tells her she might travel all day and still be told nothing, but Sophia reminds him it's a hospital, and if refused she'll put the back of her hand to her forehead—and she does so— "and swoon. Isn't that what women used to do, swoon? They'll *have* to let me in."

"Perfect," he says flatly. "It's an insane asylum," then, determined, "I'll drive you."

"I'm not riding in your truck for hours."

"I'll rent a car," he says hopefully. "A convertible. We'll take a room for a night and—"

She reaches across the small table and places her hand on his. "I must make this journey alone."

Unable to find a reply, he shakes his head, discouraged. "I love independent women."

After briskly hanging up on Sophia, Mrs. Elliot remains at the phone. When she first began working at the hospital there were occasional calls about Miss Audrey but that ended decades ago. She laughs to herself that she too has grown old now, that much of her life has been spent giving Miss Audrey care that far exceeds the position's requirements. Mrs. Elliot knew that the reasons for committing Audrey could be managed today with counselling and medications, but that was another, harsher time when even the hospital's original name was unsympathetic. Knowing that part of her duties is to shield this old woman from discomfort, Mrs. Elliot leaves the reception desk thinking how this woman on the telephone might call again.

Sophia is sure Max will give her a little time off and plans to leave in a day or two. In celebration of her discovery she and Terry walk First Avenue to East 7th Street and her favorite Indian restaurant where a thousand tiny lightbulbs hang from a low ceiling. After vegetable paratha and the doughy, butter-brushed naan that she loves, then chicken biryani all to the soft twang of a sitar, they stroll St. Mark's, lively this soft night early in June. They pass the Reggae T-shirt store and headshop, a health food restaurant with outdoor tables beneath an awning, and the dive bar Grassroots a few steps down with the best juke box in the East Village. Outside Café Orlin they order cappuccino along with almond cookies since Sophia doesn't like cake.

On a lawn chair before a narrow storefront, a woman neither young nor old with dark, searching eyes and wearing many necklaces, large hoop earrings, and a lace capon on her head. Beside her is a sandwich board sign QUEEN ELIZA and *Clairvoyant Extraordinaire*.

Gathering in the folds of her long dress of many colors, a white, embroidered fichu around her shoulders, rising slowly from her chair and stepping closer, Queen Eliza asks, "A reading for a nice couple?"

To Sophia, Terry whispers, "Let's look into the future."

"Don't the stories tell us that's unwise?"

"Maybe she can see what you'll find in Ogdensburg."

Drawing near, Queen Eliza tells them, "A special for tonight," looking to Sophia, then Terry. "Two readings for one price."

Terry has decided and imitates the Godfather badly. "She made us an offer we can't refuse," then enters her storefront. Sophia follows but whispers to Queen Eliza, "Let him know I'm not the one." The gypsy touches Sophia's arm and nods understandingly.

Inside, dimly lit by candles, incense burning in upward coils of thin, blue smoke and a crystal ball glowing from the candle behind it, at a small table covered by a paisley cloth, Queen Eliza—a ring on each finger and her thumbs, bracelets jangling—holds Terry's hand, palm upward as she traces its lines and ridges with her finger.

"Your lines crisscross." She nods knowingly, her gaze moving along his wide hand. "You have taken many roads," and she follows the lines, "and there are many roads ahead."

She looks closer, shifting her glance side to side.

"You are one who loves deeply," she utters, looking into his eyes and then his palm again, "but you must love as the hummingbird that tastes from many flowers." She closes his hand within hers, looks to him and whispers, "The sweet fields lay before you."

Turning now to Sophia who nods once quickly in gratitude, Queen Eliza unfolds Sophia's hand, gazing into it for a suspended moment before her heart surges and she sits back. The room is smaller now, a tent lit by a kerosene lantern at a county fair. Barkers call and bells jingle outside along the Midway; Queen Eliza has aged.

"You shall be famous and beloved," she whispers into Audrey's small palm, then looks at the black-haired girl with light eyes, "but happiness will turn to ashes in your mouth," as shadows tremble in the flickering candlelight, "and you shall walk in solitude for longer than you wish."

# Chapter Seven

For more than a year, Audrey had tried not thinking about the broiling tensions in Europe despite each newsstand's sandwich board—
### WAR IN EUROPE
—then a row of newspapers with ominous headlines thick and black—
### GERMANY INVADES BELGIUM
### ALL EUROPE IN ARMS

But now it seemed as if the war was drifting west like the poison gases she'd read about released over French battlefields, and she wondered irritably why Europe's problems must concern America. *Aren't they always ending some war and starting another?* And now her dear Gabriel's brooding intention of heading to Canada to enlist. Only when she reached the gated entry to MacDougal Alley did she calm somewhat amid the row of quaint, two-story houses and the warm scent of horses at an open stable door just as a border collie colored like graham crackers scampered down the mews.

In one bright, cluttered studio with high ceilings and four French doors opened to the spring day, Audrey stood upright in a simple gown, her elbow bent, her hand raised to her side and just below her chin, her index finger and thumb forming a delicate 'O'. Gertrude Vanderbilt

Whitney sat on the edge of a stool directly in front of Audrey, legs spread and feet on the floor, her white smock spackled with chalk smudges and paint drips, her black hair tied on top. Slender, lovely, she worked intensely on a mound of clay on a rotating platform just below her waist, her lively eyes traveling from Audrey's pose to the emerging clay figure.

"No matter how the newspapers ridiculed it," Whitney declared, "that armory exhibition is the future of art, and nothing can stop it."

Again Whitney's eyes moved to Audrey, then back to the clay.

"What art I've seen in Paris for a decade now will soon be made here in New York. It's another revolution." To Audrey she asked, "Are you alright, dear? Need a rest?"

"I'm fine, Miss Whitney."

"Well *I* do," and she put her fettling knife on the table. "You have the endurance of a filly."

Audrey released herself from the pose and joined Whitney in comfortable armchairs where they were served tea and fruit and biscuits.

"Thank you, Abbie," Whitney said to the tall young woman with long, brown curls and a spattered smock. After a few sips of tea, her eyes on Audrey, Whitney said quietly, "I was glad to learn you who had posed for Adolph Lukeman's memorial to Ida and Isidor Straus." She took a small, solemn breath. "As you know, those lost at sea have a special place in my heart. One day I too will create a memorial to those lost on the Titanic. To those men who gave their seats on the lifeboats," and shook her head in disbelief. "Imagine doing such a thing."

"Of course," she resumed once they were back at work, "the figure I create for *my* memorial must be a male. For true beauty, it is the male of the species. Look at the birds."

"Miss Whitney," Audrey said, "you are the only artist I know who converses while working."

"I'm the only artist you know who is a *woman*," she said while removing clay with her thumb from one place on the figure and pressing it elsewhere. "We can do more than one activity at a time, which is why *we* bear the children." She paused and looked at Audrey. "And it's *Ger*trude, my dear, please call me *Ger*trude," then returned to the clay. "Though I *am* your senior you are first my friend." After a thoughtful moment, she added, "Well, *second* you're my friend," and returned to work. "You are an artist's model first. Tilt your wrist back just a touch."

When work concluded for the day, the two women stood at the studio's front door open to the mild afternoon. Audrey wore a form-fitting, cream-colored linen dress in a floral design, a pale, nearly transparent wide brim hat in her hand, and Whitney—having changed her paint-speckled smock for a colorful silk wrap—said, "And here is a small commission," handing Audrey an envelope. "That last piece for which you posed brought us a reward."

"But Miss Whitney," Audrey said both graciously and surprised as Whitney drew back in objection. "*Ger*trude," Audrey corrected herself. "Thank you, but you already pay me more than—"

"And I plan speaking to some of the prominent *men* in the neighborhood about that," then nodded aggressively. Softening, she asked, "Are you meeting your young man today?"

"He's waiting now."

"Does he know he loves the world's most perfect model?"

"It's not a notoriety that truly pleases him."

"So he isn't an artist then?" she asked hopefully.

"Oh Miss Whitney," Audrey uttered in playful distress, "he's a *writer*."

"Dear *God,* woman!" Whitney cried, then touched Audrey's hand, "though they *are* the most passionate lovers."

The two laughed, Audrey curtsied slightly, then stepped from the doorway back into MacDougal Alley's narrow, cobblestone lane. Under the bright afternoon sun now she wore her wide brimmed hat, shadows of its lace pattern leaving thin, curved lines on her cheeks and across her nose. Since she knew only vaguely when posing for Miss Whitney might end, Audrey hurried through the gate and toward Washington Square where Gabriel casually leaned against the Arch, waiting, a hand in his trouser pocket, a soft fedora pushed back a little on his head and watching as she grew nearer with quick, light steps. And he knew he must be in love because he barely noticed other girls while waiting though some time passed watching two white butterflies in erratic flight around each other until the bushes hid the rest of their mating dance.

Audrey eagerly stepped nearer, then Gabriel came to her, his hand lightly on her back, her hand on his chest as their lips touched despite her coyness in public.

"My, don't you look lovely," he uttered with a small, astonished laugh.

"Oh so do you," she replied, lowering her chin and smiling as she took his arm before they moved deeper into the park.

The Square flowed quietly alive with other couples and hurrying students, nannies pushing prams, cars and buses rushing through the Arch, and the old man wearing a floppy sunhat sitting at his easel painting the afternoon. He was adding a child with a stick spinning a large hoop but unable to include the sound of chirping sparrows or the distant notes of an accordion.

Since the Armory show, Audrey was accustomed to people whispering in passing or a discreet, pointed finger, especially here in Greenwich Village with its many artists and studios, where paintings leaned on stoops or a fence, the shabby artist himself seemingly indifferent if someone bought. Her notoriety still mildly embarrassed Audrey, and she smiled politely in response while Gabriel struggled not to appear too smug that her arm entwined in his.

In the small yard behind the storefront bakery was a café with eight round, cloth-covered tables for two beneath strings of tiny bulbs lit even in the afternoon. The backs of brick tenements surrounding the tables rose to the sky filled with the passing sun for two hours each day along with the gentle clink into the night of cups on saucers, conversations, and the aromas of pastries, coffee, and tea.

"And it shouldn't matter when I leave," Gabriel said across from her. "On Tuesday you're taking a train to California."

Audrey leaned back in the chair impatiently.

"That I'm off to make a movie and you're heading for France are not the same."

Her eyes grew tense, and she said with conviction, "America isn't even *fighting* over there," then leaned closer again, "Why must *you*?"

After a pause, he said solemnly, "England is under attack. This is the Motherland, where my father and brothers were born."

"Then let *them* do the fighting," she cried louder than she intended, then glanced apologetically at the nearby tables while composing herself. "Besides," she added hushed and irritated, "you're *Irish*."

Her eyes impatiently scanned the café garden, then returned to Gabriel. "Can't you wait to see if the United States enters the war?"

"That will happen soon," he said with quiet assurance. "There were Americans on that ship."

"Oh Gabriel that's what I mean," she whispered again. "All those poor souls. Miss Whitney's own *brother* was on the Lusitania."

Again she quieted herself, then said with an assured nod, "At least wait until I return."

With weak laughter, Gabriel said, "The war could be over by then."

"Over by then," she muttered angrily, her eyes raised as she crossed herself. "Please make it over by then."

When she looked at him again her voice was fearful and hushed. "I can't bear to think of you in those terrible trenches."

"About that you needn't worry," he said confidently. "I'll be high above them, in the skies." He glanced briefly to the top of the tenements. "Airplanes are used in warfare now. For reconnaissance and map making."

He lingered on her pale, troubled face with patterns of her hat's lace brim like thin, curving brushstrokes across her cheeks and deepening frown. And though he would soon worry as she boarded a train for a three-thousand-mile journey west, he no longer possessed that youthful assurance of invulnerability but knew he loved her, and that fate had its own plans for them both.

Sunlight had softened as they again strolled Washington Square, shadows of full-leafed trees stretching along curved walkways and blue lawns. Amid the quiet mingling two young women passed, their arms linked, both wearing trousers and one smoking a cigarette. Audrey smiled as Gabriel's eyes followed the young, daring women.

"Did I tell you," Audrey asked excitedly, both her hands around his arm, "this used to be a military parade ground?" and she suppressed a laugh. "But all that marching time after time loosened the turf to expose wooden coffins because this was once a *cem*etery." Her eyes widened. "Isn't that ghastly?"

They laughed with the light abandon of youth until hearing "Miss Munson" from a tall, slender man with a sweet smell of brandy who tipped his Panama hat. "How much more delightful can this day become after seeing the beautiful Miss Munson?"

He tried kissing her cheek, but his hat bumped the brim of Audrey's hat, then he laughed lightly.

"Señor Scarpitta," Audrey said, then introduced "Gabriel Gavin."

"Mr. Gavin," Scarpitta declared energetically to Gabriel's faint amusement, "the luckiest man in New York," then added with a suave whisper, "you know you are, don't you? The luckiest man? You know that, don't you?"

Gabriel's amiable smile faded.

"Often I have imagined how lucky you are," Scarpitta continued. "Miss Munson has the most attractive part of the feminine form in grace and symmetry," and Audrey lowered her eyes with embarrassment as Gabriel's jaw tightened. "And you know her most alluring parts, I imagine," as Scarpitta leaned closer, whispering roguishly, "of course you do," then unsteadily to Audrey. "Those dimples on your backside. I know of no other model who has them." He leaned toward her and whispered emphatically, "Guard those dimples, my girl," then to Gabriel, "and if you ever see them going" and to Audrey again, "cut out the apple pie!"

He tipped his hat, smiled with unsteady charm, uttered, "*Buongiorno,*" and Gabriel's eyes narrowed on Scarpitta moving away to Audrey's bashful laugh as she took his arm and they strolled deeper into the park. Gabriel removed his hat, twice ran his hand aggressively through his light-brown hair, and with his irritation simmering they neared several couples dancing in the shade to a mournful little two-step squeezed and stretched from the yellow accordion harnessed to an old man's chest. Gabriel enclosed Audrey's waist with his right arm as she turned unhesitant to his gentle, guiding steps.

"What a lovely tune," she whispered, then felt the front of him warm and alive, his hand behind her pressing softly.

"It tells a sad story," he said, "of change and loss."

In their soft shuffle a little flame for him rose in her heart, a flush of love as her fingertips on his shoulder pressed him infinitely closer.

"Little Jimmy Casey," he whispered, "and Jakie Krause the baker, who always had the dough."

She felt his knee for a moment between her legs, and then again in their dancing.

"And Mamie O'Rourke, who taught us how to dance."

The soft force of him pressing in front thrilled her and she felt too the swelling of him against her thigh. With a light Irish brogue he sang softly, "*They would part, with all they've got,*" then turned his face slightly so his lips brushed her cheek and his hand lowered to just above her backside as she felt again his firmness against her, "*if once more they might walk—*"

Gabriel heard her soft, aroused breaths from parted lips as her eyes closed. "*—With their best girl, and have a twirl—*"

The accordion ceased its gentle play, couples untangled but Audrey remained in his embrace"*—on the sidewalks of New York,*" then she turned her cheek so that her lips touched his.

∽

BEFORE BOARDING THE train to California with her mother, Audrey threw an exalted glance upward at Weinman's figures of herself paralleling the great, wreath-encircled clock above Pennsylvania Station. Through the sunlit waiting rooms, the black-steel beams high above, down the long platforms followed by their luggage on hand trucks to their berths, Audrey and Kittie began the next of what continued to be unimaginable adventures.

During the long journey, Audrey read magazines and newspapers purchased at each stop along the way—Cleveland, Chicago, Denver—and from the slender volume of poetry with a dark leather cover Gabriel had given her. She watched the varied landscapes from her window, amazed at the vast prairies beyond the Mississippi River that seemed to extend forever, and as the train chugged through the Rockies, she now understood why people believe the gods live on mountaintops.

She and Kittie enjoyed long, leisurely meals in the dining car; even here Audrey was recognized though it was Kittie who was most proud. Neither slept well to the raucous rhythms of the iron wheels along the rails, at times the train shimmering terribly with loud, metallic rattles and nearly tossing them from their berths.

Three days later, the chauffeured ride from Los Angeles' La Grande Station to the boulevard of tall palm trees in Santa Barbara thrilled Audrey and her mother as Fifth Avenue had a few years before. To Kittie the excursion felt like an exotic journey to the South Seas.

Once settled in their bungalow, Audrey immediately changed into her swimsuit. It was not a dress-and-pantaloon suit—the custom of the day—but a black one-piece with its tank top upper, the rest tight along her body and down only to mid-thigh. With a frilled parasol for both style and protection from the sun, she walked the few steps to the Pacific Ocean, blue and sparkling with a bright sun above.

One morning as those perfect feet and ankles waded in the warm, white tide line, a seaplane skimmed the shore. She heard it loud and closing from behind, then watched as the black, ugly, marvelous machine passed just above the waves only a hundred yards off shore. It ascended, banked, and returned because the young pilot was equally dazzled by the lovely young woman in the provocative one-piece.

"I must fly in one of those someday" Audrey had once cried to Rozie while losing his breath at seeing an airplane circle New York Harbor during those grand, festive days five years ago.

Now her hope came true, Audrey adding to her own growing popularity as she posed in that black one-piece beside the seaplane and its dashing pilot. **"Queen of the Artists' Studio"** ran an article in that week's *Movie Weekly* **"Takes to the Skies!"** She wore untinted goggles, a leather helmet fastened beneath her chin, and a long, white scarf that flapped in the wind with her long, black hair.

Flying above the shoreline terrified and thrilled her at once, the engine loud and hideous yet the wings so fragile; surely the wind and speed would tear apart the canvas and thin, wood struts. When her fear soon abated, and with the pilot's easy glides through the cloudless sky, she imagined Gabriel as the pilot as together they shared even this small piece of his vulnerable life in France; now she could see the world as he did, and as did the birds and angels and God.

In her dream of flying with Gabriel, there was no terrible engine roar but only the wind in his airplane like the one in the photograph taped to the wall of his apartment she'd seen after their tender waltz in Washington Square. In a five-story walk-up with a tailor shop in the storefront—SHAPIRO'S CLOTHING in gold letters on its wide picture window—Gabriel had led her up a stoop, through the front door and, after a flight of stairs, his floor-through apartment where he hung his hat on a coat-tree, then lit a gas fixture on the wall. Audrey had glanced discreetly at his rooms, simple and neat—a few books on a shelf, a small desk with a huge, black typewriter surrounded by paper. There was a small, framed photograph of her at the edge on the desk, and a picture torn from a magazine taped to the wall of a British Nieuport 10, the plane seeming to her much too fragile to be so high in the clouds.

"Tea," he said, "or something else?" and he smiled; she smiled too. "Something else."

From a cabinet he took a bottle of Bushmills Irish whiskey and poured a half inch into glass coffee cups as Audrey strolled to a kitchen window. Soap bubbles drifted past, and in the small, tended yard below, a young woman glanced up at her as Gabriel joined her at the window.

"Gabriel," Audrey said hushed and worried, "to your safe return."

"Now don't fret about me," he smiled, then, placing his cheek beside hers, whispered, "I've the luck of the Irish don't you know," and swilled down his drink.

After her own thin sip, Audrey said softly, "Oh dear boy, don't you know it's a most distressful country?"

It was a night of desire, apprehension, and youthful sensuality. He was tender and tentative, she eager and a little frightened. The bedroom darkened once sunlight disappeared, and she felt both delicate and remarkable in his arms which she hadn't known were so strong. During their soft kisses she stroked his throat and along his bare chest, then down his trim waist to his erection which briefly startled her. Her body was smooth and pale and cool, and he kissed her everywhere—her yearning lips, her throat, her lips again, along her breasts each so light and lively, then down the soft, white swoop of her belly, and when she felt his kiss between her thighs she shivered.

∽

FOR THE MOVIE *Inspiration* Audrey played a city waif discovered by an artist for whom she poses nude. The director told the film crew on the first day of shooting that he expected them to act professionally despite the distractions.

"I don't want this young woman any more uncomfortable than she already must be," said George Foster Platt. He had dark hair, a strong jaw, and intense, dark eyes. "So think about your work and not what's in your trousers."

A cameraman wondered, "What about what's in *her* trousers?" and Platt told him she won't be wearing any. After the film crews' brief laughter Platt said, "Tell Miss Munson we're ready."

Audrey appeared from behind a screen in a floral robe to a set that resembled more of a drawing-room than any artist's studio she'd ever seen. The actor/artist and his actor/assistant were dressed not for working but a formal dinner. She gazed with feigned confidence at the small set, the cameras and lights and dark figures behind them, her heart beating quickly.

The director asked, "Are you ready?"

She closed her eyes, took a deep breath to brazen it out, exhaled, opened her eyes and nodded, then "Action," as Audrey gracefully stepped up on a small platform. The actor/assistant removed her robe as the camera filmed her from the side, her arms uplifted. "Hold, hold," Platt declared as the actor/artist circled her with exaggerated concern. "Hold!" Platt said again, and Audrey didn't move, barely a breath, motionless as a statue which she must retain else the production will be shut down for indecency. When the actor/artist took up his sketch pad and pencil to begin work, Platt exclaimed, "And *cut*!"

When the painting was complete—so the film script went— and the model wandered off in the vast metropolis, the artist realized he loved this woman and scoured the city to find her. Discouraged, he returned without hope to the statue of a naked, coy figure above a basin so that he might gaze again on her image, only to find the beleaguered girl, huddled and cold.

"It's based on her life," was one erroneous story about the movie. Another false story was about the sensation it had made in Paris, and though praying for Gabriel's safe return Audrey was relieved he hadn't attended the movie's release in New York. Negative publicity followed quickly, there were raids on movie houses across the country and demonstrations against the film with chants of "Exploitation not Inspiration" loudly proclaimed outside theaters. A resourceful reporter sought out Konti at his Lincoln Arcade studio who irritably declared the objection about the film entirely stupid, that nude images were found in museums around the world.

But such controversy would soon become incidental when the black clouds that had been covering Europe for more than two years now inevitably drifted west.

# Chapter Eight

Sophia catches an early morning train at Pennsylvania Station. At Seventh Avenue and 33rd Street she takes an escalator beneath a huge, hideous, drum-shaped Madison Square Garden, then passes over-lit shops under a low ceiling before boarding the train. She finds a seat by the window. After slowly winding through dark tunnels below the city, then passing factories and battered, clapboard buildings, the ride along the Hudson River is beautiful. The river is wide and gray and still, the strong, tall trees on the distant shore like Eagle River, and she tells herself that when this search for Audrey Munson ends, she'll return home a while. By now her mother's commissioned pole stands in the park near City Hall, and her father will surely rest easier knowing his daughter is safely home at least for a little while.

 She had brought Ovid to read again the story of the statue that transforms by a kiss into a real woman but the landscape compels her, that and how in some way she's always been on this journey to Audrey Munson, always drawn to what remains behind; the campgrounds once the boys left at the end of summer; the church reverberating after the pipe organ's oration when the town gathered in prayer for those astronauts trying to get home; and the empty fields and rutted lanes when the state fair left town.

Late each summer the Wisconsin State Fair comes to Vilas County pitching tents and promises on the flat pastureland south of town. With the low sun in his eyes, her father drove the family there, Wenonah beside him, her long, black hair whirling in the cab, the children in the open truck bed holding tight to the side panels and shrieking joyfully whenever the pickup hit a rut that bounced them as water splashed from rain that morning.

Booth after plywood and canvas booth along the Midway lured sharp shooters and hatchet throwers run by hard, tattooed women, flirtatious and missing teeth, their men lean and dirty with large-knuckled hands. Banjo and fiddle music spilled from one tent, WRKR from Milwaukee playing rock and roll in another, and one tent had a sweet smell of whiskey and a gambling wheel inside. The giddy rides jangled, bells rang from points racked up at Skee-Ball, a loud, metallic *clang* like in a prize fight at the strength test after a lumberjack's mighty blow. Sophia and her brothers rode the tilt-a-whirl, the roller coaster, and Ferris wheel as the sky darkened and the carnival lights grew brighter.

The day after the fair left town, Sophia threw a blanket on Billy's back and rode slowly along the abandoned fairgrounds, among the wheel ruts and trash, a muddy lane where the Midway had been. Knowing that every sound resonates forever, she listened for the faint bells and the barkers' calls and the lingering, departed spirits.

On her first New Year's Eve in Manhattan, she and Angi had ridden the F train to Times Square half an hour after the ball dropped despite Angi complaining of the cold.

∽

SOPHIA ARRIVES IN Ogdensburg that night, takes a room at the old Sherman Hotel on Franklin Street, then laughs while at the bathroom sink that has no hot water. "Just like home." She sleeps late, and after coffee and a muffin at the hotel's small café she walks the few miles to The Saint Lawrence Psychiatric Center. By early afternoon she takes the pathway to the entrance of a large, somber, two-story building of brown stone. A wide porch wraps half way around it with a turret from where can be seen the cold, swift river for which the hospital gets its name.

"Good afternoon," she says to the young receptionist at the front desk.

"Good afternoon. May I help you?"

"I'm here to visit a patient."

The receptionist is young and plump, her red hair pulled back so tightly she seems to squint because of it. "And whom do you wish to visit?"

"Audrey Munson."

The receptionist freezes a moment, knowing this is who called a few days before. "Visiting hours," she says with cool detachment, "are Saturdays from one o'clock to four."

Quietly, apologetic, Sophia tells her, "I can't stay that long, and I have traveled a long way," but the receptionist repeats the same words in the same, cool manner.

"Please," Sophia implores, taking an exasperated breath. "Is there someone I may speak to, someone who might," and she fumbles, "help?"

Again the receptionist softens.

"Have a seat," she says, then picks up the phone to call the nurses' station on the second floor.

In the quiet, sun-lit ward, nurses tend patients' needs amid a dim clatter of plates and cups. Mrs. Elliot carries a cereal bowl on a tray down the center aisle toward Audrey Munson in a wheelchair sitting at the far end of the ward by a window. She wears a long, white robe, and a toy kitten lays in her lap. A nurse sits close by quietly reading to her " 'the glory and freshness of a dream' " from a slender, ragged poetry book though Audrey appears remote as she gazes out the window.

" 'It is not now,' " the nurse recites, " 'as it hath been of yore: turn where-e'er I may' "—

" 'Turn where-*so*-e'er I may,' " Audrey corrects immediately.

" 'Turn where-so-e'er I may,' " as the nurse continues, smiling, " 'by night or day, the things which I have seen I now can see no more.' "

Mrs. Elliot places the tray on a table nearby.

"My O's!" Audrey cries in delight to the bowl.

The attending nurse tucks the poetry book beneath the toy kitty, then wheels Audrey closer to the table. Before dipping her spoon into the bowl, Audrey dabs a fingertip in the milk and softly touches each cheek while looking out the bright window.

"I should like to go—outdoor after my O's."

"Of course. Beneath your favorite tree?"

"Oh yes," Audrey says, "always in the shade. Though I love the—sunlight, nothing is worse for a girl's complexion." After a moment she asks Mrs. Elliot, "Will you join me or—will it be that nice Mr.—Arlington?"

"With whomever you wish," she replies just before the nurse adds, "With whom*so*ever you wish."

"But tell him," Audrey says with slight alarm, "to bring—more *pea*nuts this time. The squirrels won't come to me unless—I give them *pea*nuts."

A nurse stepping quietly on white, silent shoes approaches Mrs. Elliot.

"Excuse me Mrs. Elliot, there's a matter for your attention."

"Miss Audrey," Mrs. Elliot declares, "I leave you with your O's."

The nurse accompanying Mrs. Elliot to the phone whispers, "Someone at the front desk asking about Miss Audrey," which is no surprise to Mrs. Elliot, her resolve increasing with each step down the wide, carpeted stairs. She walks right up to Sophia who is watching her approach.

"May I help you?" Mrs. Elliot snaps.

"I'm here to visit Audrey Munson," she says quietly, boldly to Mrs. Elliot who is exactly as Sophia imagined her though even more displeased than expected.

Mrs. Elliot tightens her lips, nods several times while glaring with hard, dark eyes slightly downward at Sophia. "You're the one who called the other day. Her *aunt* if I remember."

Sophia laughs, weak and embarrassed but her eyes smiling.

"Why is it so important you see Miss Audrey?"

"Then she *is* here!"

"Yes, she's here and quite well but unused to visitors," then Mrs.

Elliot raises her eyebrows with condescension. "Why is it so important you see her?"

After a moment, slowly, Sophia says, "I want to see her face, look into her eyes. I want to tell her that all the beauty she gave New York City is still there and still touching our hearts." Her eyes remain on Mrs. Elliot. "I want her to know this."

Mrs. Elliot continues glaring at Sophia, eyebrows still lifted. "Why don't I just *deliver* the message?"

Her gaze remains, but looking into Sophia's eyes, so light and hopeful, and, Mrs. Elliot notices, nearly the same color as Miss Audrey's, she softens.

"Perhaps this is fortuitous," Mrs. Elliot mutters, then firmly, "Tomorrow is a little party for Miss Audrey. Hospital staff, a few patients," and she raises her eyebrows again but smiles faintly, "and *you* apparently. Tomorrow then, after her nap, about four."

Sophia places her hand on her throat. "Thank you *so* much, Ms.—"

"Mrs. Elliot," then adds pointedly, "and Miss Audrey does not like cake."

# Chapter Nine

That spring day a year before in Gertrude Vanderbilt Whitney's studio—Audrey posing upright, gowned, her thumb and index finger forming a fine 'O'—Whitney had declared with all the promise in her voice that "What art I've seen in Paris for a decade now will soon be created here" about the future that Isidore Konti had gloomily beheld at the Armory Show. But the more immediate reason for Audrey no longer posing was the Great War, this monstrous, unstoppable vacuum that kept pulling more and more into it even from the distant, bloody fields of Verdun. *All those fine young men killed,* Audrey brooded angrily. *And why? Aren't the leaders of these enemies cousins or something? Isn't the English queen grandmother to the German kaiser? Why must men do such horrid things?*

Her spirit lifted slightly one cloudy April afternoon in the Oak Room of the Plaza Hotel where she'd lunched with Konti during those ascending, more promising days. At a small banquet honoring Karl Bitter after the unveiling of his *Pomona* at the Pulitzer Fountain, she would enact statues seen throughout the city for which she posed.

"Appropriately overcast," Isidore Konti said quietly to himself while glancing at the gray sky. Rain had held off for fifty guests seated in the semi-circle of viewing stands around the fountain, Konti acting as speaker for the somber event. He told of Bitter's other acclaimed works in the city—his elaborate doors at Trinity Church, the embellishments on the Custom House—ending with the sculptor's heroic sacrifice of his own life to save his wife.

"This is his final work," Konti said, pointing to the naked goddess Pomona, coy and demure atop the fountain's central column, never mentioning that he himself had completed the statue. The fountain's architect Thomas Hastings was introduced, and after young, handsome Mayor John Purroy Mitchel spoke about the beauty that Bitter could have given the city in these dark days, the gathering trailed slowly to lunch in the hotel's elegant Oak Room. And though he had once said to Audrey, "Perhaps one day *your* figure stands outside my hotel," Henry Black was displeased.

"And she'll keep her clothes on," he snapped at Konti assertively.

"Of course!"

"Fine then," Black said. "Now let's get this girly show over with."

"Henry," Konti declared with amazement, "this is a great tribute to some of the city's finest artists, and at your hotel."

"With a stripper," Black snarled.

"With the artist's model!" Konti exploded.

In the lush dressing room where Audrey prepared for the event, Kittie muttered, "It seems with all this ceremony they could at least give you a few dollars," as she tied her daughter's long, black hair into a bun. "How are we supposed to survive?"

"Kittie," said Rozie with sullen pomp, "she's doing this for art."

"I'm doing this because Mr. Konti asked," Audrey replied lightly.

"I don't trust Italians," Kittie said.

"I told you Mommy, Mr. Konti is Austrian," which Kittie shrugged away with a muttered "or the Jews" before catching herself and turning an embarrassed eye to Rozie. "Present company excepted."

After a dismayed nod Rozie took another sip of a gin and tonic which she hoped would calm her irritation that Kittie was right, Audrey should be paid something.

In a floor-length Greek tunic, sleeveless, nearly sheer, with a plunging neckline and a dark ribbon around her waist, smiling with uncertainty, Audrey asked first her mother, then Rozie, "How do I look?"

"Lovely," Kittie said immediately, "a goddess come to life."

After a small, sad laugh, Rozie told her, "You truly do."

Audrey knew she was no longer the eighteen-year-old who had posed for *Three Graces,* but she'd become famous since then, acclaimed as Miss Manhattan, even a movie star of sorts, and surely modeling would resume again; like the rest of the country, hard times are endured until the war finally ended and everything returned to the way it was. And thankfully Gabriel would have safely returned as Audrey too glanced quickly to the ceiling.

A knock at the dressing room door startled her as if an ominous message was being delivered though she had immediately calmed herself by the time a tall young man in a red Royal Coachman coat escorted her along a carpeted hallway to the Oak Room. The gathered guests were at tables encircling a low, small platform, and on this Audrey stepped before taking the pose of *Pomona* to light applause. She straightened slowly, lifted her right arm, head tilted back, and arching slightly recalled *Beauty* from the public library's terrace as Konti told the gathering the name of each piece, its sculptor, and where it was displayed in the city. Audrey reached above her with one arm, her fist tightened, then struck the gallant pose of Weinman's *Civic Fame* high over New York

The applause comforted a nervous Kittie standing at the perimeter while Rozie's anger rose at each snicker from a table of young men with hair freshly trimmed and wearing tuxedos. When Audrey bent her knees slightly, her arms extended, one of those at the table rose from the velvet-cushioned chair and exaggerated straining to peek down Audrey's gown until Rozie pranced by and, stumbling, spilled her drink in his lap before a breathless, "*So* sorry, darling," and hurried on, "but I des*pise* rude behavior."

∽

Within a few months, what Audrey had feared she'd see soon appeared in bold headlines—

**AMERICA IN IT**
**US TROOPS ON WESTERN FRONT**

—then rations followed, and buying bonds, and smooth-faced soldiers wearing fresh uniforms marching in regiments along Broadway.

*"Send the word to be heard over there—"*

One chilly, bright afternoon Audrey knocked on Gertrude Vanderbilt Whitney's Greenwich Village studio allegedly to say hello but hoping to find some work posing. Whitney's slender assistant was very happy to see her and invited her in for tea but "Mrs. Whitney is still in France" and seems determined, Abbie told her, "to remain there until every soldier in her hospital is sent home."

*"—and we won't come back 'til it's over over there."*

No longer posing and with no money coming in, Audrey and her mother moved from their beloved West 77th apartment into one room on the second floor of a boarding house on 65th Street far on the west side. Its owner, Doctor Walter Wilkins, lived with his wife in the large first-floor parlor, and Kittie immediately detected the portly, bearded, middle-aged Wilkins' lecherous eye for Audrey who saw only the dull boarding house and their dreary room.

"With a good cleaning," Kittie assured her, "we'll be fine. And when you start posing again, you're even closer to the Arcade Studio," then kissed her forehead. "Now buy fresh flowers" and gave her a nickel "and I'll put on the kettle."

Adjusting to their descending circumstances wore at both Audrey and Kittie despite Kittie's effortful optimism. Whatever profits from *Inspiration* seemed quickly entangled with litigation from lawsuits and, to Audrey's mind, stolen by Jews who run the movie business. Just as Kittie knew that Audrey had once been the reason for their good fortune, she now blamed her daughter for their growing hardships even while knowing it wasn't Audrey's fault at all. Still, Kittie's irritation rose each time she left three days a week to serve as a housekeeper in uptown mansions on Riverside Drive.

Now it was Audrey doing the laundry at the kitchen sink, keeping the one room apartment clean and unaware that each time she entered the boarding house after doing the shopping, the Wilkins' apartment door opened slightly just as she began climbing the stairs. She was not the first young, female tenant that aroused the landlord, but when Wilkins discovered that Audrey was hardly another young, pretty tenant, the lyrics *"And loving her simply means that I'm busy buying magazines"* drifted continually from his Victoria Victor phonograph. Again and again through that slightly opened apartment door, the lively notes from the piano carried down the carpeted hallway as he watched Audrey who was unaware that his gaze fastened on the shifting swells of her bottom with each step up the staircase.

One November afternoon as the city celebrated the Armistice with giddy, grateful joy, Audrey sat across from Rozie at a small table in a narrow bar on West 38th. Despite the jubilation, Audrey was troubled and nervous. Rozie watched her with concern as an old waiter placed a cocktail on the table.

"Nothing for you?" Rozie asked. "If those church marms in Nebraska have their way we won't be doing this. At least legally."

"Tea," Audrey said to the waiter as Rozie raised her glass, declared, "To peace," then after a sip said with conviction, "Of *course* you can do this. You're a better model than me and I've posed hitting a golf ball for Coca-Cola, showing my foot for Keds, and with," shaking her head, annoyed, "*stuff* all over my face for Stillman's Freckle Cream." After a quick sip, Rozie added angrily, "And paid better than those famous artists ever paid you."

"When I posed," Audrey whispered with rising anxiety, "I was Virtue or Beauty, and I certainly don't have your cover girl smile."

Rozie considered this as Audrey's tea arrived, then, "You could advertise hats for Altman's."

Audrey, sat back, incredulous. "Hats for Altman's?"

"Elsie Janis does and you're far prettier," then she sang, " '*Florrie is a flapper, so dainty, so dapper.*' "

Suddenly animated, Audrey leaned closer. "Gabriel wrote that he saw her perform in a boxing ring in a French town. She ends her show doing *cart*wheels!"

Rozie shook her head in mild amazement, then said tenderly, "Half the men in America are in love with you and you're waiting for Gabriel Gavin. You're such a romantic." In a poor Irish brogue, she asked, "And how *is* the fine lad?"

He's seeing much of France, Audrey said, though he wrote only of its beauty from the sky and the kind, appreciative people. When he sent the letter the Armistice hadn't yet been agreed to, but he believed "the war must be over soon" though didn't write that it would end because there were simply so few young men left to kill.

"The wounded are coming home first," Audrey said, "so he must wait," and she smiled shyly, "to have a twirl with his best girl."

Rozie snapped a glance at the small timepiece on her narrow wrist, then "We must go. You have an appointment." Audrey reached into her purse. "No, you'll pay next time."

For two hours Rozie accompanied Audrey to advertising agencies, each gazing with disinterest through Audrey's portfolio. In one photograph she resembled a Greek goddess holding a candle-lit bowl, in another she sat on a riverbank wearing a revealing gown, and one of French's *Miss Manhattan*.

"Miss Munson," the agent said, smiling apologetically, "your friend Miss Spear is a fine client of ours, so I agreed to see your photos. Miss Munson, no one takes photographs of goddesses anymore. Something different is coming after this awful mess in Europe. The world has changed," and he returned her portfolio with faint superiority. "These images are the past."

In Times Square the two women jostled through crowded, hectic streets as buses filled to the double-deck slowly rolled along a choked Broadway. Tipsy people danced awkwardly around a pyramid ten-feet high made of German helmets, while others sat astride the barrel of an artillery piece, a gin bottle raised.

"I don't *want* to do this modeling," Audrey cried barely audible above the commotion. "It's not even modeling," she sneered. "When I pose, I hold it for longer than a flash in a pan."

Only now did she gaze at the theater lights and the marquees' bulbs and again felt the rush of panic that the spirit of her bright destiny had abandoned her, disappearing like the steam rising from manholes. "*When you think that happiness is yours*"—the gypsy fortune-teller had prophesized.

"I'm an artist," Audrey cried while throwing a wild, painful glance upward to a **BUY BONDS** poster above Broadway, "not a manikin holding toothpaste."

In a loud, urgent whisper, Rozie said, "I was merely hoping you could get a little money."

Amid jostles and discourtesies Audrey muttered loudly, "Always the money with you people," and immediately sensed Rozie recoil. Audrey glanced at her, gave an apologetic nod, and after an awkward embrace they each took a different subway home. They would never see each other again.

༄

WITHDRAWING INSIDE HERSELF with the best and richest part of life seemingly having vanished, Audrey grew isolated from the world and troubled more by no longer posing than hints of age. She knew her earlier radiance had dimmed, a hollow sensation dropping from her throat with each recollection of French's *Memory*. She felt a looming sense of apprehension for her future which had only recently seemed so bright. A dull fear continually pressed down upon her white shoulders; perhaps revealing herself in *Inspiration* really *had* been a transgression as some said it was. *Is that why the guiding spirit has abandoned me?*

Though Audrey remained unaware of the eyes watching her climb each stair, Wilkins' wife knew, and she'd known about the others as well; now there was this new bewitchment. Through the thin floorboards

Audrey and Kittie heard the muffled shouting that happened, so it seemed, nearly every day, and Kittie suspected the reason. During those unsettling quarrels she barely heard the doctor, but his wife's voice, hard and assertive, told him, "I'm no old fool" and "you don't think I know" and "I'm tired of this." A door slammed, and there were long lulls before Mrs. Wilkins' voice again carried upward.

Their fiercest quarrel—when even the doctor could be heard—happened one morning after Wilkins collected the rent.

He had watched Kittie leave for the day, climbed one flight up and tapped lightly at their door. Audrey opened it tentatively and gave a weak smile to the doctor who said through a suave, lewd grin, "That time of the month again."

"Yes, of course," Audrey muttered, then hurried to a small desk. With the door slightly open Wilkins took an assertive step inside before gazing pleasurably at garments drying on a line above the sink. Audrey returned with an envelope; Wilkins counted the cash, took a receipt book from his suitcoat pocket and wrote one out.

"I suspect these are not easy times for you," he said, then leaned closer, "but there is a way you could make good money" if she posed for him, privately, that it would be well worth her efforts. She explained uncomfortably and with slight belligerence that she posed only for artists, but Wilkins declared, "Here is a chance to expand your talents," adding, "and you might save a great deal on rent. Will you think about it?"

Though vaguely disgusted Audrey nodded, then closed the door and retreated into the apartment where she heard, "What is this again?" from Mrs. Wilkins standing in the hallway. "I told you *I'm* collecting their rent," she demanded as music from the phonograph wound out the apartment door—*"as I love her on the cover of a magazine"*—and Wilkins, calm and decisive, said, "You won't keep me from" as their front door slammed like a pistol shot.

Three days later a detective knocked at the door "investigating the disappearance of a Mrs. Julia Wilkins." He was tall, thin, in a dark, vested suit, wearing a hard expression and a black derby. He asked

Audrey when was the last time she'd seen Mrs. Wilkins and if there were any recent disturbances.

"What is this about?" Kittie demanded, and the detective showed a postcard advertising photograph found in Dr. Wilkins' suitcoat pocket of Audrey on a pedestal wearing the black swimsuit.

"There are pictures of my daughter in a *dozen* magazines," Kittie laughed uncomfortably. "She's the girl on the covers you've been seein'."

When Kittie nor a baffled Audrey had any more information to give, the detective said firmly to "notify the police if either of you sees Mrs. Wilkins."

Two days later Kittie hurried into the apartment. "We're leaving. We must pack at once," then to her daughter's startled eyes declared, "It seems the good doctor has been charged with murder, and as sure as the day is long people will find *you* the cause of it. We're leaving."

"But I don't *want* to leave," Audrey cried.

"Well you didn't want *this* to happen either, now did you?" Kittie then pulled two suitcases from beneath the bed. "There'll be inquiries," she said, "the papers'll write about you, show photos, that bloody movie will be dragged in." She stopped, turned to Audrey and, with her hands on her hips, uttered tenderly, "It's no matter that you're innocent, my love, because the press will make quite a show of it."

Stunned, Audrey asked, "Where are we going?"

"Back to Rochester," and she tossed a suitcase on the bed. "We still have family there, and there we can disappear from this bugaboo of suspicion," then Kittie turned to Audrey with finality; "Now pack your bloody bags!"

∽

AUDREY SENT NO exhilarating glance upward at the statues of herself as *Day* and *Night* paralleling the wreath-encircled clock above Pennsylvania Station. She feared the sight would only make her situation seem more terribly unfair as she fled New York as if in shame, but why she didn't understand.

Her father still lived in Rochester though Audrey could remember little of the large, remote man and only the town's dark warehouses and a cold wind blowing across Lake Ontario. Kittie had maintained brief, infrequent contact with Edgar Munson over the years; that way Audrey might have some ties with her father as well as for Kittie to occasionally borrow money despite Edgar's own struggles as a trolley driver. As the train passed slowly through a tunnel beneath the Hudson River and headed west, Audrey kept thinking about a lesson from her years at the St. Francis Academy. But to her this was no Sodom she fled where a dozen statues of her through the city were made not of salt but of stone and marble and bronze. *Lot's wife was punished for what I'm doing now* as the train rolled toward Rochester and Audrey looked back in sorrow.

Rochester was a seven-hour train ride, but Audrey could neither read from the thin poetry book nor sleep, her heart racing each time she tried dozing off with returning thoughts of this dreadful scandal as she woke in a panic.

Her estranged father had found Audrey and Kittie a furnished room in a boarding house a half mile from town. Though quietly admiring his daughter's notoriety and success for the statues of her throughout New York, *Inspiration* troubled him; her likeness in stone or bronze were often vague, but the movie revealed her undeniably, her name across the poster, and these protests against the film, the theater closings, and now this entanglement with some landlord. **Artists' Model Sought in Wilkins Inquiry**, he'd read in *The New York Sun*. As he'd been doing nearly all her life, Edgar remained distant and so added to Audrey's dismay.

At last she wrote to Rozie passing off the hasty departure on Kittie's sudden urge to see her old home again. Audrey *so* missed New York and was already making plans to return though such plans remained unclear both to Rozie and Audrey. Rozie quickly replied but mentioned nothing of the news articles regarding Dr. Wilkins which she'd surmised was the reason for Audrey's flight. Rozie had found that Greenwich Village apartment with her sister Ruthie near Abington Square just below West 14th Street "that allows dogs *and* Jews." There was a day bed "anytime you return to your kingdom," though Rozie never heard from Audrey again. And it was Edgar who informed Kittie after reading in the June 30, 1919, *New York Tribune* that Dr. Walter Wilkins—found guilty of first-degree murder and sentenced to the electric chair—hanged himself in his prison cell. With vague sentences and few facts, Kittie told Audrey about the shocking event, adding quickly, "And though it's a terrible thing," and she crossed herself while glancing to the ceiling, "the Lord punishes the wicked." Despite sorrow for the doctor's wife and even his own terrible fate, Audrey hoped that this troubling matter would soon be forgotten so that she might return to New York.

Late one morning in her best coat, Kittie entered Rochester's Memorial Art Gallery on Prince Steet carrying a cloth-covered object one-foot high. In the museum director's office, she unveiled a white, marble bust of Audrey, hair tied high on her head, "Carved by Daniel Chester French," Kittie said, adding, "who did the great statue of Mr. Lincoln, you know." She let a moment pass, then, "He gave this to my daughter as a gift."

As the director's gaze moved along the piece—the strong profile, the extended neck, the smooth, white eyelids— Kittie said hopefully, "Perhaps the museum might display it," and after another pause, added, "The model her*self* could pose beside it and the museum could charge a few coins for the exhibition." She spoke again after a moment, hurriedly, less assured. "Perhaps share the profits with the model," then, "minus expenses, of course."

The young, pale director replied slightly distraught that "the museum might exhibit the piece" though it seemed unlikely for the model to pose, "particularly with her present," and he hesitated, "notoriety," then laughed uncomfortably. "We don't want a mob of the curious storming our small gallery." He gazed again at the lovely carving, then with weak optimism said, "But leave the bust and we'll see how it might be exhibited. Let me write you a receipt."

Believing that her daughter's fame in New York City would embarrass Audrey if her mother needed a job, Kittie pressured Audrey to find something that will "tide us over," she declared, "until you start posin' once again." But Kittie now feared that perhaps those brighter days would never return, that their lives were becoming the future Audrey had seen in that mirror she held once and focused behind her, then Kittie shuddered when hearing again the gypsy woman's foretelling. *"Happiness will turn to ashes in your mouth."*

Audrey applied first at the public library on South Avenue where she most wanted to work though it needed no one at the moment. Nor did a small pet shop where cages of melodious canaries and squeaking bungies hung from the ceiling. *How nice*, she thought, *to work among these little animals*. While she was speaking to a department store's clothing and accessories manager, a woman on the other side of a glass display case said loudly to the man beside her, "Look Charlie, there's that awful woman who takes off her clothes for money."

It was the single most horrific moment in Audrey's life. She immediately grew weak and couldn't breathe, and for a moment felt as if losing her balance. She looked at the smirking face but refused to cry, instead lifting her chin and hurrying from the store, returning no one's glance.

"But I *never* took off my clothes for money," she cried to her mother that night. "I'm an *artist*," in growing alarm. "Why don't people realize that?"

"That bloody film," Kittie muttered, then angrily, "and the ugly crow would probably do the same as you did and for less than *you* were paid."

The unhappy evening passed—though Audrey went to bed in their shared room without patting her face with milk— but after the incident at the department store Audrey turned self-conscious in public and a little afraid of the world. She thought people pointed at her but not as they had in New York; there were no "Miss Manhattan" or "American Venus" but only women whispering together at the market, scowls and crooked fingers. Men passed with lewd glances or else simply stood staring. Often, she remained huddled in her room where she felt chilly even on warm days, and everything troubled her; she was angry she wasn't back in New York City at the start of such a rich, exciting decade, irritated with no letter from Gabriel so long after the Armistice, and she hated this dreary town and their dismal rooms.

On other days she'd gallantly stride outside with colorful scarves tied around her forehead and neck as she had when posing in Felix Herzog's photography studio but looking even more bizarre pushing a rickety perambulator she used to wheel home groceries. She didn't notice she was talking to herself until laughing so loudly she froze, self-conscious and silent, then, with chin uplifted, she continued on her way while singing a song from her chorus girl days all the more precious with thoughts of Gabriel—

*Take me up up up, with you dearie*
*Away up to the sky . . ."*

She sensed the scowls indiscreetly thrown at her and felt a hot flush of pain and rage if she thought a woman whispered something about "clothes" again, but rising above it, above it all—brazing it out, she laughed—she kept singing,

*"Sail around the moon for a quiet spoon*
*Just the parson you and I . . ."*

She flipped one end of a scarf over her shoulder, then bought a penny-bag of peanuts from a shabby vender with tired, kind eyes. They chatted amicably of the mild weather before she moved on, hoping this showed how she was quite fine. On the tattered lawn a squirrel hopped near, then sat up, front paws together as if begging, and to Audrey the little creature seemed more pure and unjudgmental than any living thing in Rochester. She tossed a peanut that it snatched off the grass. To her delight another squirrel appeared though her attention instantly fixed on a man scolding his leashed dog and striking the cowering little animal with a cane.

"What are you doing there?" Audrey shouted at him, hurrying closer while pushing the wobbly carriage. The small, fat man—frozen by her words—stared in shock.

"Someone should take that cane," Audrey hollered, "and beat *you* with it!"

She quickly realized that others on the sidewalk stared not at him in equal outrage but at her with a kind of shock. After a deep breath, she threw a handful of peanuts at the man before hurrying home where Kittie knew there'd been trouble.

"What is it?"

Audrey yanked items from the wicker carriage and set them on the table while muttering, "This awful man hitting a dog."

Relieved but irritated now, Kittie declared, "And you said something. Audrey, you must *stop* this. Last week that wagon driver nearly took his whip to *you*!"

Audrey removed from the carry bag a small brick wrapped in wax paper. Kittie's eyes brightened.

"Butter!" her gaze briefly lifted to the ceiling. "I think I missed butter more than heat. Oh it *is* fine that bloody war finally ended," and, smiling, "which reminds me."

From her apron Kittie took a blue, wrinkled envelope. "This came for you in the post. Perhaps your young man is coming home soon."

Sullen, Audrey took the letter. "It's only been a year since the last one."

"Well don't be beatin' too hard on the lad," Kittie said. "The letter must've taken some time tracking you down all over New York City and finally here."

After a quick kiss on Audrey's forehead, she said, "That Jew butcher won't carry pork but has the best chicken at the best prices," and left the apartment with eager flurry. Within an hour Kittie stood terrified over Audrey who was face down in bed, her naked body soaked with perspiration as Doctor Stone rubbed her down repeatedly with a cloth.

Hushed, desperate, Kittie asked, "She'll live, won't she?"

"Yes," he replied, irritated, glaring at the small brown bottle of mercury bichloride in his hand. "Had she waited another few minutes for it all to dissolve she would have gotten what she apparently wanted."

What she apparently wanted came peacefully seventy-five years later, at the age of 104, in The St. Lawrence Psychiatric Center, a blue-gray cotton shawl across her lap that February afternoon in 1996. But Doctor

Stone knew more about the human heart than what he detected through a stethoscope, that sometimes people don't want to end their lives but only hurt themselves the way life kept hurting them. He covered Audrey with a dry bedsheet to her black, tangled hair while hearing notes from a distant piano faintly play a light, little tune and thinking *she's young and probably pretty* as Kittie muttered, "I can't handle her anymore, I can't handle her anymore," and Doctor Stone wondered what demons could have led her to this.

If Doctor Stone could follow those same, soft piano notes played years before at the St. Francis Xavier Female Academy in Providence, he'd see the tall, pretty girl with black hair and blue-gray eyes who loved music and dance classes where she learned to move gracefully as the little tune returned in a varied pitch, wavering along the piano keys that roll to the Rocky Point Amusement Park—and Queen Eliza's prophecy "*when you think that happiness is yours . . .*" before hopping, pausing, and then skipping to—"None of them twenty" calls the barker through a megaphone, "None of them married"—Girlies at the New Amsterdam Theatre in New York City, the high-notes tingling across a small stage where a young man dressed like a peppermint stick sang and danced,

*"She has the love of every fella,*
*oh yes she does, let me tell ya,"*

then reached out to the audience,

*"Egyptian El-la."*

He bowed repeatedly to light applause, then, "Last night," his thin cane twirling, his derby hat cocked to one side, "one of these next young lovelies kept beating on my hotel door for hours until I let her out." Then to a few weak laughs, "Thank you, thank you," and again bowing in excess. Suddenly, a snare drum roll. "And now," he cried, arms outstretched while fading stage right, "the New Amsterdam Theatre is tickled to tantalize with the talk of the town, those heart-breaking hoofers from heaven, The Dancin' Dolls" who tap-danced in a line from stage left, Audrey among them all in ruffled skirts to that same light piano music Doctor Stone could hear only now accompanied with eager applause.

AUDREY AND HER mother had embraced New York as if they'd entered a magic, iridescent kingdom. Audrey was still a little unbelieving that she danced on Broadway, but even a small part in a small show from Providence brought her ever closer to becoming her dream as a Ziegfeld Girl. The city was vibrating with activity, a place of continual wonders, a new, thrilling encounter around each corner. Ever-taller buildings seemed to have risen within weeks above the dense, busy streets where women demanding the right to vote marched up Fifth Avenue—a boulevard with mansions each like a castle, where finely dressed people strolled as if in a familiar dance and beautiful horses pulled elegant carriages. Before the towering spires of St. Patrick's Cathedral, Kittie crossed herself and whispered eagerly to her daughter, "And it's Irish!"

In a few blocks they walked West 58th Street, the elegant Plaza Hotel before them like a piece of wedding cake though yet to receive its stirring artifact above the fountain's basin still unfinished only steps outside its grand, canopied entrance. To their left, an iron-gated mansion as large as a palace; surely, Audrey thought, this must be American royalty. Even the young woman and her two male companions leaving the palace seemed endowed with a special aura as slender Gertrude Vanderbilt threw a brief, genuine smile through the gate at Audrey watching the three who seemed to possess all the casual grace and wonder of Manhattan.

But ever-protective—especially in this wonderland where everything seemed suspiciously possible— Kittie had noticed a trim, well-dressed, middle-aged man following them for two blocks with an intense eye on Audrey. Pausing before a shop window, Kittie watched in the reflection of the glass as the man slowly walked by, lingered steps away and returned.

"And what, sir, is your business?" Kittie asked in challenge, then added with a touch of sass, "If you don't mind me askin'."

Though slightly startled, he quickly recovered, then gave a cordial, "Good afternoon," while tipping his hat. "Photography is my business," he said, then asked Audrey if he might make a few photographs of her face. "You'll be paid, of course," then handed her a small card. To Kittie he said, "Felix Herzog," and tipped his hat again. "Please come, both of you, to the studio anytime tomorrow for tea." As he continued along Fifth Avenue, Audrey and Kittie stared after him in bewilderment, then turned to each other with incredulous smiles.

Felix Herzog's studio was among many in the newly converted Lincoln Arcade Building on Broadway off 66th Street at the northern edge of Hell's Kitchen and becoming known as Uptown Bohemia. Audrey and Kittie entered a large, bright loft where a dozen young women sat on long sofas and upholstered chairs near tables of fashion magazines. For the next three afternoons Audrey posed first alone, then with another young woman, then three, Rozie among them, their foreheads and necks wrapped in colorful silk scarves, the large, black camera close to their faces with Herzog, hooded, behind it, images of the young women upside-down. After the first day and certain Herzog was a genuine photographer, Kittie remained at home where Audrey headed one afternoon when a hurrying man ahead of her bumped a young woman so forcefully that her handbag spilled to the sidewalk.

"Hey," Rozie yelled to his wide, fleeing back, "watch yourself, ya big lug!"

She bent to gather the contents of her bag as Audrey did too.

"Well *thank* you," Rozie said, "aren't you a dear," then adding with irritation, "I des*pise* rude behavior."

When the brief task was done, she held out her hand as commuters hurried by and said, "Rosalyn Spear, but call me Rozie."

"Audrey Munson, but call me Audrey," she laughed. "Do you live this way?" Audrey asked and pointed, but Rozie didn't. With faint disappointment, Audrey said, "I'm going uptown" and Rozie smiled. "I can tell that, sister."

Each was momentarily reluctant to leave, then Rozie tilted her head toward Central Park nearby.

"Walk awhile? We can work out the kinks from all those poses," and they entered the park late that cool September afternoon, passing the vigorous construction of the *Maine Monument*, its pylon rising block by granite block.

"What in heaven," Rozie cried to the top of the tower, "will they put up there?"

Audrey too looked up at the rising tower. "Nothing I could dream!"

Within only a few moments Rozie knew that Audrey and her mother had arrived in the city three months earlier and was thrilled to be with a Broadway star.

"Not yet," Audrey laughed, "but in another week," and Rozie laughed with her. "You don't have to be very talented," Audrey admitted with shy humor, "just pretty. We do some mechanical steps, smile a mechanical smile and stay in a mechanical line."

Audrey suddenly stopped beside a green, rolling meadow where a hundred sheep grazed. "Sheep?" she cried, astonished. "And we're in the middle of Man*hat*tan?"

"They even have a shepherd," Rozie told her, a bemused eyebrow raised.

*Here*, Audrey thought, *is another in this city of unending wonders* as Rozie called, "Hurry on now," and looked over Audrey's shoulder, "your mothers are worried" as two boys in knickers fled in the opposite direction and both young women laughed.

"Now, *you're* from New York," Audrey said to Rozie as they resumed their stroll.

"Willett and Delancey Street," Rozie replied, "in the same apartment where I was born, and my older *sister* was born," then with a small, affectionate laugh, "and my *younger* sister. Poor Papa," she said in smiling resignation. "Three daughters and he makes men's trousers."

She and her older sister Ruthie were looking for their own apartment in Greenwich Village though "It's mostly Italians and they don't like Jews either."

She shook her head in dismay, adding, "No Jews, no dogs."

Audrey wondered if she'd ever met a Jew and how Rozie was unlike anyone she would think Jewish. She nearly asked if that were her real hair but thought it too intrusive, then with exaggerated distress, "Why not dogs?"

Rozie flinched an instant before Audrey smiled and Rozie laughed, "Now aren't *you* a character!"

At the photography studio the next day, Herzog gave Audrey a note. "Please take this upstairs to Isidore Konti's studio."

Konti's studio was vast, meant not for photographs of exotic models in scarves but statues in clay, plaster, and stone. White dust hung palatably in the air and lit with a pale glow from large, cloudy windows above scaffolding and shelves, thin ladders leaning against brick walls, tables of half-completed figures and several busy workers.

"Mr. Konti, please," she asked one passing.

Soon Konti appeared in a dusty apron, his face, like the studio, hazy with powder. "What is it?" he asked, impatient.

"From Mr. Herzog," she answered apologetically while handing him the note.

He read that the young woman delivering this message had a particular talent in addition to her beauty and perfect proportions. *And Isidore*, in Herzog's splendid penmanship, *she may prove valuable for your recent commission.*

Konti lifted his eyes to her and softened. In the days ahead he would tell Kittie that "Every beautiful woman must contribute what she can to art and loveliness," and to this Audrey would dedicate the fullness of her young, strong heart.

# Chapter Ten

That night in Ogdensburg's Sherman Hotel, Sophia sleeps restlessly, the windows dark each time she wakes until a pale glow finally appears behind the heavy curtain. In her fitful sleep she imagines Audrey as she appears in the statues–her full cheeks, her eyelids like seashells—but at a window, gazing down at a small tenement's yard when bubbles appear and Sophia laughs herself partly awake with thoughts of Angi.

Two hours before the gathering, Sophia sits beneath a large oak tree near the hospital of brown, solemn stone, its wrap-around porch and single, solemn tower. The lawn is green and full this late spring afternoon, and in the near distance beneath a tree she watches an old woman in a wheelchair feeding squirrels from her outstretched fingers. A young man lingers close by. One squirrel scampers away as another approaches the old woman.

From her pack Sophia takes a sketch pad and a narrow, tin pencil box and begins sketches of the hospital though thinking all the while that soon she'll be near the woman who posed for the familiar statues done over seventy-five years ago. *Seventy-five years,* and Sophia takes a breath, *a long lifetime of its own*, then lifts her eyes to a mild, blue sky and to fate, blind and inexplicable.

Before long Sophia puts the pencils and sketch pad in her shoulder bag, then hurries to the hospital's entrance. Now she is nervous. The young receptionist from the day before smiles softly in greeting and, expecting her, calls upstairs. Soon a nurse leads Sophia up the wide, carpeted staircase to the second floor, bright from its many windows, her heart beating rapidly. At the far end of the ward, a small group gathers near an old woman in a wheelchair, her hair long and white, a bathrobe nearly to her slippered feet, then Sophia's lips part for her faintly audible breaths.

Audrey looks with slight uncertainty at Sophia, then to the nurse and back to Sophia.

"Hello," Audrey says. "Do I—know you?"

"Miss Audrey," says Mrs. Elliot, "this is Sophia."

Sophia reaches her hand to Audrey who, after a brief hesitation, extends her hand.

"Nice to meet you," Sophia says softly.

"Nice to meet *you*."

Sophia looks hard into Audrey's bright eyes before exchanging comfortable nods with the few others at the gathering, but she looks again at Audrey while realizing with a mild shock that the woman who posed for those statues throughout the city is a real woman after all, that here she is this woman who is the woman across New York, that here is the real Miss Manhattan. Yet as captured as she is at seeing Audrey, it is Audrey's voice that holds Sophia, a delicate voice, like a confident, polite adolescent, with pauses at unexpected places.

"And where do—you live?" Audrey asks Sophia.

"I live in New York City."

"Oh I did *too*," she says eagerly. After several small nods, Audrey adds, "I always liked New York City," and her glance slowly trails along the hospital ward, "but I live—here now."

A cart arrives with milk and cookies, sliced strawberries and plump, red grapes, and a narrow vase with a lavender tulip. In one cookie is a small, thin candle.

"A candle—for each century," Audrey says joyfully.

Mrs. Elliot lights it.

"Make a wish," a nurse insists.

Audrey closes her eyelids like seashells, lifts her chin and smiles. "A bottle of champagne—and an airplane ride" then opens her eyes. "It's the same wish—every year," then blows out the candle with a small, quick breath.

During the quiet applause, the small chatter and the serving of treats, Audrey feels Sophia's soft gaze. Audrey smiles faintly in return, tilts her head to one side and, with less uncertainty, asks, "Don't I know you?"

Sophia can't explain the many times they've been together in New York, about her search and even now can't tell her why, only, "Yes you do."

Each person at the little gathering has a gift. The attendant nurse gives Audrey a Mason-Pearson hairbrush which Audrey removes from its box and brushes her long hair while declaring, "This is the finest brush I've— ever used." Mr. Arlington gives an elaborately wrapped bag of peanuts, and from Mrs. Elliot a hardback copy of *All Around the Town: A Walking Guide to Outdoor Sculpture in New York*. On the cover, a glossy, colored photo of Weinman's *Civic Fame* atop the Municipal Building. Sophia is momentarily astonished at seeing the book she'd taken from the library months ago but knows these things happen along such trails. After a long moment Audrey taps the book several times with her fingertips, then with a quivering lip lifts her eyes, glistening and happy, to Mrs. Elliot who says, "Maybe there's one or two you'll recognize."

Audrey again looks at the book with her golden figure high over Manhattan and whispers, "Maybe one or two."

Sophia removes her scarf and with it encircles Audrey's shoulders. A little bewildered, Audrey pets the scarf, then delicately with her fingertips spreads out the fabric to reveal the library's façade with *Beauty* in the alcove. She raises first her eyes and then a hand to Sophia. "I *do* know you," she says, and as their hands touch Audrey looks through the open window. In the distance, a small, single-engine plane high above, solitary, silent.

# *Epilogue*

Audrey Munson died at Ogdensburg's St. Lawrence Psychiatric Center in February 1996 at the age of 104. Only the *Ogdensburg Journal* ran an obituary which incorrectly stated she had married (the alleged groom's name misspelled) and only that she had posed for the 'Liberty dime' though Audrey was but one of several models for the coin. Her remains were cremated according to state law, the ashes interred on her father's plot at New Haven Cemetery outside Oswego, New York. There would be no headstone for twenty years, and the one finally placed had her birth date wrong.

But her gifts to New York City endure. In the portal on the terrace of the New York Public Library's main branch on Fifth Avenue, her *Beauty* is sensuous and pale each summer, cold and fragile in the winter. *Pomona*—completed by Isidore Konti after Karl Bitter's untimely death—stands with coy modesty atop the Pulitzer Fountain outside the Plaza Hotel. The Firemen's Monument at Riverside Drive and 100th Street with Attilio Piccirilli's *Duty* and *Sacrifice* has become a yearly gathering site for collective mourning each September 11. His three figures for which Audrey posed still grace the *Maine Monument* in the southwest corner of Central Park, and Augustus Lukeman's figure of her in Straus Park at Broadway and 106th Street still dreamily gazes above the fountain;

there's a ceramic tile of this memorial on the platform of the 1 train at 86th Street.

Audrey modeled for the lounging figure in the pediment above the entrance to the Frick Museum at 1 East 70th Street. She also posed for the central figure atop the Manhattan Appellate Courthouse on East 25th Street off Madison Avenue though its face is too weathered to be recognizable. Adolph Weinman's *Civic Fame* at the golden peak of the Municipal Building on Centre Street remains the tallest statue in Manhattan. The sensual figures of *Day* and *Night* he carved that once paralleled the enormous clocks at the original Pennsylvania Station now parallel a wreath at the Eagle Scout Memorial Fountain in Kansas City, Missouri. One figure of his *Night*—rescued from a landfill in the New Jersey Meadowlands—is displayed at the Brooklyn Museum of Art where *Miss Manhattan* and *Miss Brooklyn* by Daniel Chester French remain enthroned on the museum's terrace. *Memory* and *Mourning Victory* also by French are in the American Wing of New York's Metropolitan Museum of Art, and Audrey very likely posed for his *Spirit of the Water* displayed in Gallery 770. Adolph Weinman's most alluring *Descending Night* is in Gallery 768.

Except for a plaster copy in the Hudson River Museum in Yonkers, what became of *Three Graces*— Isidore Konti's marble figures that began Audrey's brief reign as Queen of the Artists' Studio—remains a mystery.

www.ingramcontent.com/pod-product-compliance
Lightning Source LLC
LaVergne TN
LVHW041606070526
838199LV00052B/3010